Secret of Abbott's Cave

Max Elliot Anderson

Secret of Abbott's Cave

Tweener Press

Baker Trittin Press
Winona Lake, Indiana

Secrete of Abbott's Cave
By Max Elliot Anderson

Printed in the United States of America
Cover Art: Paul S. Trittin

Published by Tweener Press Division
Baker Trittin Press
P.O. Box 277
Winona Lake, Indiana 46590

To order additional copies please call (574) 269-6100
or email info@btconcepts.com
http://www.gospelstoryteller.com

Publishers Cataloging-Publication Data
Anderson, Max Elliot
        Secrete of Abbott's Cave - Tweener Press Adventure
Series / Max Elliot Anderson - Winona Lake, Indiana
Baker Trittin Press, 2004

                p.   cm.

Library of Congress Control Number: 2004110908
ISBN: 0-9752880-0-8
        1. Juvenile   2. Fiction   3. Religious   4. Christian
        I. Title   II. Secret of Abbott's Cave
JUV033010

Dedicated
to the true heros
everywhere.

Chapter 1

Randy Wilcox lived with his family in New Market, a little town in Virginia. Their house sat along a tree-lined street in an old established part of town. Some of the houses in his neighborhood were built before the Civil War, but Randy's wasn't that old.

All things considered, Randy had it pretty good. He enjoyed a loving family, and he lived in a beautiful part of the country called the Shenandoah Valley. Clear rivers and lush green hills surrounded his home. New Market was such a little place with nothing very far away.

Randy abruptly awoke to the sound of a heavy truck rumbling up his street. "Could that be it?" he wondered right out loud.

He rolled out of bed and stumbled to the window of his upstairs bedroom. Randy's room faced out toward the front of the house, so he could easily observe anything that went on in the neighborhood, unless it happened in the backyard, of course.

The sound grew louder as the lumbering truck drew closer

to Randy's house. Then it stopped in front of the house next door.

"Come on," Randy complained, "I could make out the name on the side if we didn't have that overgrown oak tree in the yard. Wouldn't you know the truck would have to be coming from that direction?"

Finally, the large gray truck pulled up right in front of his house and stopped, blocking the driveway. Its bright yellow warning lights flashed like something out of a science fiction movie.

Randy's light green eyes darted toward the truck, straining to read the name.

"Oh man," he groaned, "I forgot. This is our garbage pickup day."

What a disappointment. Now he would have to wait a little longer for the most important delivery of his life. He had placed the order about a week ago, but he and the guys were too cheap to pay for next day delivery. The shipping company promised ground service on his package in seven to ten days. This was only day eight, but it felt like eight months to Randy.

And the guys?

Stewart Adkins looked like a guy who had never met a dessert tray he didn't like. His rounded features matched his large bushy head of hair.

Jeff Stevens and Hal Conti were about the same size and both had short black hair and dark eyes. Jeff liked to pick on the others sometimes.

Three of the friends were eleven years old. Randy was the

oldest. Hal's birthday was still a couple months away.

These were Randy's friends but not just any friends. These guys had formed the Hilton Park Road Detective Club. Together they planned to help solve crimes.

Randy was president. Besides being a good leader, one of the reasons he won the election was because he was the only one with a broken down shed in the backyard that they could turn into their headquarters.

Randy ran a long extension cord from the house out to the shed so they could have electricity. That figured to be very important once that package arrived.

Why does it have to take so long? he thought to himself. *I can't stand it!*

He decided that since he was already up, he might just as well go on downstairs and see what he could find for breakfast. His mother was there preparing for a busy day of caring for her family. Most of the year she taught second grade at New Market Elementary.

"Good morning," she greeted in her usual cheerful voice. "Why are you up so early? It's Saturday."

Randy hadn't thought about that. He usually liked to sleep in on Saturdays.

"I heard a truck and thought it might be making a delivery," he groaned.

"A delivery?" his father asked as he walked into the kitchen. He wore a thick plaid shirt, blue jeans, and leather boots. Under one arm he carried a heavy jacket and a hard hat. "The day a garbage truck starts making *deliveries* is the day we pack up and move out of this neighborhood." They all laughed.

"Well, I'm expecting a package, that's all."

Rufus, the family's lop-eared basset hound, slept soundly on a big rug by the back door. Even with all this commotion he never moved a whisker. Rufus was the smartest one in the house this morning. At least he knew when to sleep in.

The rest of the detective club members weren't expected until around ten for their regular weekly meeting.

"I was hoping to announce some big news for the guys this morning."

"I forget," his father responded. "What exactly is it you're waiting for?"

"I want to surprise you, so I'm keeping it a secret. I mean the guys know what it is. They helped pay for it."

"How much did this thing cost you?" he inquired.

"A hundred and seventy-eight bucks."

"You paid a hundred and seventy-eight dollars for something without asking us first?" his mother challenged.

"Hey, I could have bought one for three hundred forty-nine ninety-five. That thing had enough power to do just about everything except my homework."

"Where did you order it?" his father asked.

"I found it on an Internet auction."

"Tell me you didn't use one of my credit cards," he warned.

"No, of course not," Randy assured. "We all went down to the post office and bought a money order. I think that's why the delivery is taking so long."

"How do you know you can trust this Internet person? You might as well kiss that money goodbye," his father said.

"Wait a minute. We're going way too fast here," Randy cautioned. "I didn't use just my money. All the guys pitched in. We used money we had saved from our allowances, for one. Jeff used some money from his paper route, Hal collected cans, and Stewart . . . well, Stewart's mother just gives him money if he asks her for it. The auction seller has a four star rating from other customers, so I think our money is in good hands."

"What could possibly be so important that you decided to spend that much money?" his mother pried.

"Could we wait just a couple more days? I'd really like it to be a surprise," Randy pleaded.

"All right," his father agreed, "but just make sure you let us know."

"I will."

"Remember, this family is based on honesty and trust. It might have been a better idea if you'd talked with us first," his mother added.

"I guess so. I just thought it was different this time since the whole club pitched in. Can I be excused? I want to go out and get the shed ready for our meeting."

"Okay," his father responded. "I'm going out to take some

readings around Broadway and Timberville. We think there might be part of a cave complex out there. Want to come along?"

"No thanks, Dad. Maybe some other time."

"Oh right, your meeting."

Randy's father gathered up his things, stepped carefully over Rufus, went out the back door, climbed into his pickup truck, and drove away.

His father worked for a company that had something to do with geology and minerals. Randy wasn't exactly sure what it was, but he had gone with him into caves a couple of times. Randy liked exploring almost as much as he liked detective work. To him the perfect job would be a cave detective, but he'd never heard of a job like that.

There were several caves in the area around New Market. Some of the most famous caves in the country were not too far from his front door. Many of them were still privately owned, and occasionally a new cave entrance was discovered on private property. This was also an area where some important battles took place during the Çivil War, especially the Battle of New Market.

Randy's shed needed a major clean up. He was so busy getting it in shape for the club meeting this morning that it seemed like the rest of the guys arrived in no time.

"Did it come yet?" they all asked.

"No, not yet. I thought the delivery truck was coming this morning, but it was only the trash man."

"Hey," Hal protested, "I hope you didn't spend our good money on trash."

Randy shook his head. "That's almost as funny as what my dad said. Trust me. We're all going to be *very* happy when it gets here, especially me."

"Isn't it time to start the meeting?" Jeff asked.

"Yes. As president of the Hilton Park Road Detective Club, I hereby declare the meeting open. First order of business is the treasurer's report. Stewart?"

"It sure isn't the best report we've ever had," Stewart complained.

"Yeah, we had around two hundred dollars last time," Hal remembered.

"Anyway, after spending the hundred and seventy-eight dollars for our order and the fifteen dollars for shipping and handling, we've got exactly twelve dollars and eighty-eight cents," Stewart sadly reported.

"Okay, the next order of business is to decide if we're going to take the caving class at the park district next week. Any discussion?"

"I have a question," Hal declared. "Since Jeff's uncle already has a cave on his farm, why can't we skip the course and just go on out there?"

"Well, there are rules you have to follow. We don't know anything about cave safety, and I know of some people who got in trouble for taking rocks out of a cave. We just need to make sure we know what we're doing," Randy replied.

"Does it cost anything?" Stewart asked. "We're down to just about a big fat zero here."

"It's three bucks a head," Randy reported.

"Three bucks?" Jeff asked. "Let's see. Three, six, nine . . . that comes to twelve dollars."

"*Twelve dollars?*" Stewart gasped. "That's going to bring us down to a grand total of eighty-eight cents by my calculations."

"Well, what good is money if you can't enjoy it?" Randy asked.

He looked around the room. "Let's put it to a vote. Remember, majority rules. All in favor raise your hand."

Randy held his up first. Then one by one all the others raised theirs, everyone, that is, except Stewart. He could get money from his mother any time he begged for it, and yet he was the biggest tightwad of the group.

"I count three 'yes' and one 'no.' The motion passes," Randy reported. Then he added, "If there aren't any questions, we'll meet again next Saturday at the park district's office for the caving class. I'll call a special meeting as soon as the package shows up on my doorstep."

Chapter 2

Randy and the guys not only went to school together, they attended the same Sunday school class at church. During the school year the boys actually saw each other almost every single day since their detective club met on most Saturdays. They often worked together on projects for school and helped each other out from time to time with their Sunday school lessons.

That's the reason why Jeff called Randy.

"Hello."

"Hi, Randy. Jeff here. Have you looked at your assignment for church this Sunday?"

"Not yet. I thought I'd tackle it tonight. Why?"

"Well, I just wondered how many times we have to learn about the same dumb stories over and over again. Can't they come up with anything new?"

Randy thought about it for a second then said, "I thought I was the only one who felt like that. Sometimes it seems like our teachers are just babysitting us."

"I know, and Mrs. Ralstead turned out to be the worst one

so far. I really hated that wretched perfume she dumped on."

"I wonder what this new guy is going to be like. We've never had a man teach our class before, so Mr. Roberts is going to have his hands full," Randy suggested.

"We should at least give him a chance. I think I could do a better job of teaching than some of the people they've thrown at us," Jeff complained.

Sunday morning the guys sat in the back of the class. Their new teacher hadn't come in yet.

"I wonder if he's going to try to act like a big kid, so we'll like him," Hal scoffed.

Just then a tall slender man with thinning hair and dark rimmed glasses came in the room.

"Oh no," Stewart pleaded in a whisper. "Tell me *that's* not him."

"Good morning children," the man greeted them with a warm pleasant voice. "Please take your seats. Mr. Roberts is going to be a few minutes late, and he asked me to get the class started."

The children settled into their chairs just as another man stumbled into the room. He had messy hair, dirt smudged on his face, and ragged, dirty clothes.

"Is he a homeless person?" one of the girls whispered to Randy.

"I don't know," he whispered back.

The man ambled slowly around the room looking at each child individually. Then he turned to the man at the front of the room and asked in a loud voice, "Where can I get something to eat?"

"This is a church," the thin man answered. "You'll have to leave now before I call for security."

"Security!" the intruder laughed in a booming voice. "That's a good one. I thought this whole place was supposed to give people some kind of security."

Then he moved toward the door, turned around, and took one more sneering look at the class.

"Thanks for nothin'," he said in a huff and abruptly left the room.

The children began to talk wildly among themselves.

"Did you see that dirty man? Eeeeeuuuuwwwww," one girl squealed.

"I thought he was going to start a fight," Jeff added.

"They should be more careful," another boy demanded. "I don't think people like that belong in our church."

Just then the door opened and the same scary, dirty, homeless-looking man came into the room again. A couple of the girls shrieked and covered their eyes.

"Good morning, class," he said. "My name is Mr. Roberts, and I'm your new teacher."

Now the children didn't know what to think. Their new teacher thanked the man who had helped him with his little charade and excused him. After the door was closed, Mr. Roberts admitted, "I don't know about you, but I get a little tired of the same old Sunday school lessons taught in the same old boring way time after time."

Jeff and Randy turned, looked at each other, and shared a knowing smile.

Their teacher took some wet paper towels out of a sack and began to clean his face and hands.

"I'm planning to teach this class a bit differently than what you've been used to. At first you might not like it, but I want to send you home each week thinking about life in a little different way."

Everyone sat in stunned silence.

"When I first came into the room, you probably thought I could be dangerous. I'm sure some of you thought that a person like me didn't belong in church. Over the next several weeks we're going to discover how much God loves every person. He sent His son, Jesus, for everyone. It doesn't matter to Him what we think might be wrong with other people."

By now Mr. Roberts had the attention of the entire class.

"Today, our lesson is about the blind beggar. That man had been unable to see for his whole life. Then he met a special person who would change his life forever. Can anyone tell me who the blind man met?"

No one raised a hand.

"Come on now. We all have to enter in if you want to learn anything."

Randy cautiously slipped up his hand. "He met Jesus."

"That's right. And what did Jesus do?"

Jeff raised his hand. "He made some mud and put it on the man's eyes and told him to go wash it off in a pool. Then he could see."

"Yes," Mr. Roberts answered. "When the blind man was able to see, he became extremely grateful to Jesus. Why do you think he felt like that?"

"He didn't have to beg anymore," a boy volunteered from the back of the room.

"Right again, but it goes much deeper. I want to do a little experiment to help you understand what the blind man experienced."

Mr. Roberts walked over and turned off the lights in the classroom. Randy and the others could still see a little because there was light coming in from the hallway through a window at the top of the door.

Their teacher took a large piece of poster board out of a paper bag. It was rolled up and held with a rubber band. After the rubber band was removed and the poster board unrolled, Mr. Roberts used some masking tape to hold the poster board in place to cover the glass. It was still possible to see faintly in the room from the sliver of light that squeezed in under the door. Mr. Roberts took out two pieces of cloth and stuffed them under the bottom of the door.

"Now, close your eyes tightly if you want to fully understand the lesson today."

Everyone did as he instructed.

"Keep your eyes closed while I count to twenty-five. As I'm doing that, just imagine that you can no longer see. The blackness will be all you know. Is everybody ready?"

"Yes," the children answered in unison.

Mr. Roberts proceeded to count, and when he reached twenty-five, he said, "Okay, open your eyes."

Randy opened his to discover a darkened room. "Hey," he said, "I can't see anything."

Others in the class made similar comments.

"Correct," their teacher responded. "What did you expect, a miracle?"

The children roared with laughter.

"Here we go then. This time I want you to believe that you are going to be able to see. Close your eyes again, and on the count of three, open them right away. One, two, three."

At that instant, everyone in the class opened their eyes. As they did, Mr. Roberts turned on every light in the place.

"Hey," Stewart yelled, "that really hurts my eyes." The rest of the class squinted as their eyes adjusted from darkness to light.

"That is exactly how the blind man felt. The difference is that you were only blind for a few minutes. He had been blind for a lifetime."

Randy knew right then that he was going to like this new teacher a lot.

"Ready for another experiment?" Mr. Roberts asked.

"Yes," they answered with excitement.

Their teacher took out four blindfolds. Several children raised their hands and began straining in their chairs hoping Mr. Roberts would choose them. "Me!" one of them shouted. "Pick me! Pick me!" others begged.

"If you look under your chair, you'll find a sticker with a number." The children jumped out of their chairs to search for the sticker. The room bristled with excitement as one-by-one the numbers were found.

"Before class this morning I came in early to put those numbers under your chairs. I've already selected the winners. First, I need number seven."

"I have number seven," a girl squealed.

"I need number twelve."

A second girl had that one.

"Three."

Stewart jumped out of his seat. "That's my number!" he screamed.

"And the last one is five."

Another boy proudly produced that sticker.

"Here is what we're going to do, and I need help from everyone in the class." He looked at Hal and said, "First, I'd like you to take our four victims, I mean contestants, into the hall so we can get the room ready."

By now Randy's curiosity was aroused. Once the contestants were gone the teacher explained what was about to happen. They would be brought into the room one at a time. Each would get a chance to take one last look at an elaborate maze created with chairs, a trash can, some boxes, and a couple of small tables.

"The surprise," he told them, "will come after the contestant is blindfolded."

The room was arranged and Mr. Roberts asked Hal to bring in the first victim, one of the girls. She listened to his instructions about memorizing the maze before being blindfolded.

She studied the pattern before her. Then the blindfold was placed over her eyes, and she was led back into the hallway. Each of the contestants had the same experience. After they all had seen the maze and returned to the hallway, the rest of the class quietly removed everything from the path.

"Are you ready?" Mr. Roberts asked.

"I think so," a timid voice replied from the hallway.

She was brought into the room, and Mr. Roberts called out, "Ready, set, go."

Very slowly the girl began to move across the room. She crouched down and felt her way along. Others in the class could hardly contain themselves and some of the children started to laugh. Finally, she made her way to her friends who were waiting on the far side of the room.

Everyone cheered as she removed her blindfold. To her amazement, the entire floor had been cleared. This game continued and finally it was Stewart's turn. He came into the room and tried to act like he could handle anything.

As he began to inch his way through the maze Randy could tell that Stewart was trying as hard as possible to get through it perfectly. When he reached the other side, he exclaimed with pride, "See, nothing to it. I knew I could get across and not touch a thing." When Stewart's blindfold came off, Randy noticed that his friend was embarrassed and his face turned bright red.

"Let's put the room back together and return to our seats," their teacher instructed. "As we conclude today's lesson, I want us to remember that God created us in a wonderful way. He gave us many unique tools to enjoy His creation around us. We can see, touch, smell, taste, and hear the world He has given us to live in. I want you to be especially thankful this next week for these gifts God has provided."

One of the other boys raised his hand and asked, "What happens if one of those things doesn't work?"

"Well, consider this. God gave us two eyes. If one goes out, we have a second. The same holds true for our ears. He had an amazing design. He made it so if one of our senses shuts down others become even more sensitive. If you lose your hearing, then your eyes take over. Lose your sight, and your sense of hearing and sense of touch kick in. The main point for this week is to notice, as the Bible says, that we are fearfully and wonderfully made."

Just then the chimes sounded signaling that Sunday school was over, and it was time to head for the church service. For the first time Randy could ever remember, the kids in his class groaned and complained that the Sunday school hour had gone by too quickly. He was already looking forward to coming back next week, but for now Randy was going to think about how thankful he was that both of his eyes worked. Only today, it seemed as if he could already see more clearly.

I don't ever want to be blind, he thought. *I hope that never happens.*

Chapter 3

Monday rolled around and it was time to start a new week at school. Randy and the guys jostled around in the hall by their lockers before their first class. The conversation centered on their great Sunday school teacher, Mr. Roberts.

"Why can't our regular teachers at school be as good as he is?" Stewart grumbled. "Man, we'd be all the way through high school before we knew it."

"So Randy," Hal said changing the subject, "do you think it's coming this week?"

"I sure hope so," Randy sighed, "because I'm getting pretty tired of you guys asking me about it every day."

"Yeah, well, I still think we got ripped off," Stewart charged. "That thing is never coming. We probably lost all our money."

Just then the bell rang and they scurried to class. Randy had become more than a little concerned. After all, he found the seller on the Internet, he was the one who convinced everyone else to chip in with their hard earned cash, and now it was up to him to come through for the rest of the club.

When they got to their science class, a message was waiting for them on the board.

ASSIGNMENT: *Research and report on a subject related to the caves of Virginia.*

"Hey, Randy," Jeff said, "this is perfect. We can find out everything we need to know about caves before we go exploring, and we get credit for it."

"Let's talk about that after school."

At the end of the day the guys got together near the soccer field. They sat in the bleachers to talk about their research assignment.

"This is a special meeting of the detective club," Randy announced. "We need to divide up the work, so we don't report on the same thing."

"Yeah, that would sure be dumb," Jeff groaned as he rolled his eyes.

"I wrote these topics down during study period," Randy told them. "See what you think. We want to find out about what kinds of caves there are around here, how many we have, and what they're made of. That's one topic. Next, I think it would be good to discover what kind of critters live in caves, so we'll know if there's anything dangerous to look out for."

"I heard bears and wolves and rattlesnakes live in caves," Stewart said in a quivering voice.

"Well, that's what we need to find out. One of us should report on cave safety. That way we'll know what to bring. We also need to know about the rules in a cave."

"Rules?" Hal asked. "You mean there are rules even in caves? I'm not so sure I want to go exploring in a place that has rules."

"There probably are some, and we need to know them. There, that's it. I've written the subjects on slips of paper. I'll fold each one in half and then we'll draw for our topics."

Randy mixed the four slips of paper around in his cupped hands. Now it was time to draw.

Stewart went first.

"Critters!" he exclaimed. "Why did I have to get critters? Some of those creepy crawly things scare me to death."

One by one the others chose a slip of paper. Jeff got rules, Hal picked safety, and Randy took the remaining slip which meant he would report on cave locations.

"That's it for the meeting. I wanna get home and start my research," Randy said.

The boys headed off in the direction of their homes. In a small town like New Market there wasn't much need for many school buses. The boys rode their bikes to and from school.

Randy turned into his driveway, parked his bike at the side of the house, and went inside.

"Mom, I'm home."

"Randy, is that you?"

"Yes, Mom."

"Come to the kitchen. Something came for you today."

That was all Randy needed to hear. Maybe all these days of waiting would finally pay off.

He dashed down the hall and into the kitchen. There on the counter was a plain brown box with a simple white label on top. It was addressed to Mr. Randy Wilcox, 237 Hilton Park Road, New Market, Virginia.

"It's here. It's finally here!" he yelled.

Randy grabbed the box and ran to his room. He got on the phone and called Stewart, Jeff, and Hal.

"Get over here right away. It's here!" he reported.

By the time he finished the third call, Jeff was already ringing his doorbell.

"Let me see it. Let me see it," he pleaded.

"We need to wait till everyone gets here; then we'll open it together in the shed."

They waited on the front step until Hal and Stewart came screaming into the driveway on their bikes.

"To the shed," Randy ordered gleefully.

Everyone was so excited they chattered like a flock of birds as they sprinted toward the clubhouse. Once inside, Randy placed the box in the center of the table. He took a jackknife out of his pocket and split the plastic tape that sealed the package. Then, one by one, he opened the flaps of the box.

All they could see inside at first were a bunch of green styrofoam peanuts protecting the contents. Randy plunged his hands under the surface of the chips and exclaimed, "Got it."

He pulled out a dark black object wrapped in clear plastic.

"It's bigger than I thought," Jeff said.

"Enough talk," Stewart nagged. "Let's plug that sucker in."

Randy unraveled the power cord. "Somebody pull the extension over here, will ya?" he asked.

Hal brought the yellow cord over to Randy. He plugged the object in and suddenly the display panel lit up.

"Wow, that looks so cool," Jeff said.

Randy flipped on the main switch and a voice crackled, *"Copy, 52."*

"10-4," a voice answered.

"What was that?" Jeff asked.

"I don't know yet. I printed out a list of what all the codes mean, but it's up in my room. I didn't think we'd hear anything so soon."

"Man, I can't believe it. With that police scanner we can hear about everything that goes on in this town," Hal suggested.

"What kind of detectives would we be if we didn't have one?" Randy asked.

About an hour later Randy announced, "Look, that's enough for now. We have to get going on our reports. I'll leave it out here, and we can mess around with it more at the next meeting. I want to get in a little research on the Internet before dinner."

Reluctantly they all agreed. It's just that they had waited for so long and now that it was finally here, there wasn't enough time to enjoy the new scanner.

Randy walked back into the house and went straight up to his room. He started working on his research about cave locations in the state, but more importantly, what caves could be found right in his own backyard. It surprised him how much information there was on the subject, and soon an hour had already passed.

"Randy," his mother called from downstairs. "Dinner time!"

"Be right down."

He bounded down the stairs and into the dining room. His father was already at the table. Randy sat down just as his mother brought in the baked potatoes.

"Let's pray," his father said. "Our heavenly Father, we thank you for this day, for your protection of each one of us, and for the delicious food you have provided. Amen."

"Randy has some news for us," his mother reported as she passed the first dish.

"News? What news?"

"A package arrived while he was at school this afternoon."

"You mean *the* package?"

"Yes, Dad."

"So what did you get? Is it some kind of a finger printing kit?" his father probed.

"Something much better. It's a police and fire department scanner. We can even dial in airplane pilots with it and hear the state police, if we tune to the right frequencies."

"You mean you can listen in on radio transmissions?" his father asked.

"Yes. We can't talk back to anyone with it though. We'll just listen in when there's a big fire or when a crime is happening. It's our way of learning how the police do their work and the ways they catch crooks. That's what our club is all about anyway."

"Well, I don't know," his mother objected.

Randy's father turned to her and assured, "I don't see how listening in can cause any trouble." Then looking back to Randy he added, "Make sure the scanner doesn't get in the way of your school work. If your grades drop, even a little bit, that thing is history. Understand?"

"I understand. Me and history have always had a hard time together."

After dinner, Randy could hardly keep from thinking about the new scanner. He wanted like anything to go out to the shed and turn it on, but right now he needed to look up information for his report. He made a quick call to the others to make sure they were doing the same thing.

Nothing ever happened in his little town anyway. He didn't think he'd be missing much action, and there would be plenty of time to listen in later.

Maybe sometime he really would hear something big. He might even use the information to help solve a crime one day.

Wouldn't that be something? Randy thought.

Chapter 4

By the time Saturday came, Randy had already reminded the other club members why the park district's cave class was so important.

"We can get information for each of our reports, and at the same time we'll find out everything we need to know before our own cave adventure," he had told them.

That morning all four boys came cruising on their bikes into the gravel parking lot of the park district's office at about the same time.

"Remember," Randy instructed, "take notes on only the information that's a part of the subject you'll be reporting on at school. Hal, you're doing safety. Jeff, you've got rules, and Stewart, you need to learn everything there is to know about critters."

"I already know everything I need to know about critters," he complained. "I know I hate all of them. There's nothing out there I trust, and I'm afraid of anything that moves."

"You can't write a report like that," Jeff said.

"Okay then, why don't you do critters and I'll do rules."

"Sorry, bud. We already drew for it, remember?"

"Well, if I find out that bears and wolves hide in caves, you can include me out of any exploring."

"That's why we're here," Randy reminded them.

They parked their bikes in the rack and went into the building. The entire Shenandoah Valley had been the site of such vicious battles during the Civil War that the park district divided its time between tending some of those areas along with the caves that were in its jurisdiction.

The instructor was a park ranger from a real cave. He had a *Smokey the Bear* hat and everything. He worked for the U.S. Government, and his assignment was the caverns at Luray, Virginia.

"I'm happy to see so many in attendance today. Cave exploring can be a lot of fun, but caves are extremely dangerous places at the same time," he warned.

The guys looked over at Stewart who appeared a little uncomfortable at the moment.

"We're going to cover a wide range of information today, so I've printed copies of my notes for you to take home and study later. Our subjects include general information for beginning cavers, cave safety, cave animals, and the many different caves you can find in this part of Virginia."

Perfect, Randy thought. *That covers all four of our reports.*

The ranger proceeded to pass out a stack of papers to each person. "I'm also glad to see some younger faces in the class today.

It's important to learn this information at an early age. That way you'll form safe cave procedures that should last a lifetime. If you pay attention, that will be a longer lifetime not a shorter one."

Some of the older people laughed.

"Going into a cave is serious business," the ranger cautioned. "It's the people who take it lightly that get hurt. Some have gone exploring and never came out."

"Oh great," Stewart whispered.

The ranger used several slides to help give a thorough presentation. Last summer Randy's science class went on a field trip to Luray Caverns. The beautiful formations and colors impressed him throughout the tour. He remembered that the entire cave route was well lighted. Handrails and steps made the trek easier. He also remembered that vast areas of the cavern weren't open to the public.

I'm sure there aren't any marked paths in most of the caves around here, he thought. He was right about that.

The cave on the farm Jeff's uncle owned could best be described as a wild cave. People knew about it, but its entrance wasn't open to just anybody who came along. A person had to have permission if he wanted to go in.

Good thing we have Jeff for a friend, Randy thought.

The instructor continued. "In this slide we see an excellent example of both stalactites and stalagmites. This also shows the importance of wearing a helmet for protection. One minute you might be looking down at something on the cave floor, and the next thing you know there's a hole in your head," he noted. "Other safety guidelines can be found in the material I prepared for you."

There were maps of the caves in the area. The ranger was careful to spell out the items every caver should have with him at all times. Randy especially liked it when the ranger said, "There are three main rules you need to follow while exploring any cave. Take nothing but pictures. Leave nothing but footprints. Kill nothing but time."

Randy could see that the guys had their work cut out for them. There was much more they needed to know before ever setting foot in their first cave. The ranger talked about the many hazards concealed in a cave's darkness.

"If you lose your light source, it's almost the same as being suddenly struck blind."

Randy remembered how good he felt about having Mr. Roberts as his new teacher in Sunday school. His demonstration of blindness made the need for safety in a cave seem all the more important.

The instructor's presentation held everyone's interest. Before long, it was time to go.

"Take your stuff home and study it this week. We'll go over what we've learned at the next club meeting," Randy said to his friends. "If you want to come over and listen to the scanner this afternoon, we can get together in the shed around three."

Everyone agreed and then rode off for lunch.

A little after three o'clock they arrived back at Randy's

house and went directly to the shed. When the boys walked in, Rufus ran out. Randy was already out there and had flipped on the scanner, but it had only made a crackling sound. No voices were heard.

"Anything yet?" Hal asked.

"Not yet," Randy said as he picked up the papers from the earlier cave class. "There's a bunch of good information here. We might even be able to move our cave day up a couple of weeks. Jeff, do you see any problem with your uncle if we decide to come early?"

"I don't think so."

"Okay." He was about to continue when they heard a voice on the scanner.

"301 to station."

"301 go ahead." The guys had learned that the man at the station was called the dispatcher and the officer calling in was known as Adam and some number.

"I have a 10-83 at 702 Jefferson. Request a 10-21."

"10-4," the dispatcher replied.

Then the scanner went silent again. Even so, four sets of eyes were riveted to the blinking lights on its face.

"What's it mean?" Jeff asked.

Randy flipped through his pages of printed police codes. "Let's see. A 10-83 is a disabled car. A 10-21 means a wrecker."

"So is a 10-4 an accident?"

"No, it just means okay."

"Wow," Hal exclaimed, "that was amazing."

Everyone agreed. All, that is, except Stewart who appeared visibly unimpressed. He blurted sarcastically, "Oh boy, a broken down ol' car. Yeah, that's really some excitement I got for my money. You betcha."

"If you don't like it," Jeff shot back, "I'm sure we could scrape together enough money to buy you out of your part of the scanner and out of the club for all I care."

"Hey, guys," Randy interrupted, "a week ago we had no idea what went on in our town. Now today, at least, we know what happens if your car breaks down. I mean there probably isn't anything around here the police don't know about. Now if it happens, we get to know about it too."

"That's right," Hal added, "and didn't you say we can listen to other police too, Randy?"

"Yes, we can. That's where the real action will come from I bet."

"Okay, so we can listen in on all the stuff that's going on in town," Stewart griped. "I just hope nothing ever happens at my house 'cause my mom would kill me if the whole town knew about it."

"You worry too much about too many things, Stewart."

"Yeah, well you would too if you lived at *my* house."

They all sat by the scanner for the next hour and a half but nothing exciting happened.

"Is this as good as it's going to get?" Hal asked.

Randy picked up the book included in the box with the scanner. "I've been reading the manual that came with it," he assured them. "We can tune in those other places too."

"Like where?" Hal asked.

"Says here we can listen to airplane pilots and the fire department."

"We don't get too many 747s landing in New Market," Jeff joked.

"Maybe not, but we're supposed to be able to listen in on the state police frequency. I'm sure there's a lot more happening out on the Interstate."

"Did any of you get a chance to look over the notes we got from the ranger?"

"I checked out some of the pictures for my section. Once I saw all the bats and the creepy crawly things that live in caves, I started thinking cave exploring might not be such a good idea," Stewart whined.

"Is there anything you aren't afraid of?" Jeff asked. "I think that would be a much shorter list."

"I looked at my stuff too. The main thing it said about safety," Hal reported, "is you have to bring a lot of lights. We need to make a list of some of the things we can find at home and what we'll need to buy."

"We gotta buy more stuff?" Stewart complained. "Man, this club is really getting expensive."

"At least you don't have to earn it like the rest of us," Jeff claimed.

"I don't care," Stewart fired back. "I could practically have a new bike by the time we see the inside of our first cave."

Randy thought for a minute, "That reminds me, Jeff. Have you cleared it with your uncle so we can even go in his cave?"

"Oh sure. No problem. It's right on his farm like I told you before. He won't care."

"Okay then, think of the things we'll need. We can each make a list and then compare them at our next meeting. You might as well bring any flashlights and batteries you have then. I think if we pool our resources we'll probably have everything."

"That's it then," Randy told them. "Let's break up for now. We need to spend some time on our research projects for school. I'll let you know if I hear anything in the next few days."

"I hope so. Otherwise I can think of a hundred things I'd rather have than a scanner that doesn't pick up anything in a town where nothing big has happened since the Civil War. Probably never will," Stewart predicted.

Chapter 5

Today's club meeting was the most important since they first voted to buy a police scanner. This would be the last time they would meet before the first official cave exploration by the Hilton Park Road Detective Club.

"Jeff, since it's your uncle's property and since your subject is safety, why don't you go first?" Randy asked.

"Okay. I learned all kinds of stuff about things to watch out for and what you should bring with you. Here, I printed out a check list for everyone."

"Thanks," Stewart sighed, "I didn't want to write a bunch of junk down anyway."

"Now I know we won't all have everything on the list, so make sure to mark down how many you *do* have of all the different things."

Everyone agreed.

"Light is the most important thing in a cave. The sun can only give light near the entrance. Once we're inside, it will be blacker and darker than anything we've ever seen."

"Kinda like what Mr. Roberts showed us about blindness?" Hal asked.

"Even darker. We need to have flashlights. If you drop your light and break it, you'll be left in the dark again. So we have to have a main light, backup lights to the main light, backup batteries, and candles. We couldn't possibly have too much light with us."

"What's next?" Randy asked.

"They say never to go into a cave alone, but that won't be a problem since we'll be together. You're supposed to always tell someone you're in the cave too. That way if you don't come back out on time, people will know to start looking for you."

"That's a good idea," Randy said.

"There's another thing. Caves are cold places. We should wear warm clothes. Also we each need a large-size garbage bag. You can put them on to keep warm and to block out water. No tennis shoes! Go home and dig out your hiking boots, the best ones you've got."

"Any questions so far?" Randy asked. No one said anything so Jeff continued.

"We need food and water in our backpacks. Food for body heat and energy and water for when we get thirsty."

"Didn't you just say we needed plastic bags to keep water away from us?" Stewart asked.

"Yes."

"Then why don't we just drink the cave water?"

"Two reasons. We don't know if we'll find water at a time

when we might be thirsty, but there is a bigger reason than that. You won't know where the water in a cave came from. It might have chemicals or some of the crud from the cave might get in it."

"No kidding!" Stewart warned. "Wait till I tell you guys about what bats do in caves. All I can say for now is you'd be better off if you bring your dad's hip boots." Then he laughed.

"The one thing I don't know about is helmets," Jeff added.

"Wait," Randy exclaimed, "I have an idea."

He walked over to some boxes in the corner of the shed and pulled something out. "My dad does a lot of construction and survey work. He has all kinds of hard hats in this box." Randy opened the flaps and took out four of them.

"I'll ask if we can use these. They're old and they've been out here for a long time."

"Those might work," Jeff observed, "except there's a problem. The main light you're supposed to have in a cave has to be one in your helmet."

"Then I've got another idea," Hal suggested. "We can take some of that duct tape and stick on a flashlight."

"That's a great idea," Jeff said. "Since Stewart is so afraid of the dark, he can strap one on each side of his helmet."

"I just might do that. Like you said, Jeff, we can't have too much light. In fact, I'm not going to have anything in my backpack except flashlights and batteries!"

They all laughed. There seemed to be no end to the things Stewart could be scared of.

"Just make sure we have some candles along and waterproof matches."

"Where do we get waterproof matches?" Hal asked.

"I know how to make matches waterproof," Randy assured. "My dad taught me."

"So how do you do it?" Stewart asked.

"Simple. You just take regular matches or you can use wooden ones. Then, you have to light a candle. You put the matches in one hand and hold the candle on its side in the other hand. The wax drips onto the match heads. When it cools, it gets hard and seals the match heads. When you need to use one, you just strike it extra hard so the wax scrapes off. You could even drop them in water and they'll still work."

"Randy will take care of the matches, but I think we should each have a lighter too," Jeff added. "That's about it. The rest of the things are on your checklist."

"Good job, Jeff. At least I know we'll be safer now," Randy complimented. "Hal, your report is cave rules. Why don't you go next?"

"My report for school will probably have some of the same things that Jeff has for safety, but I found information about how we're supposed to treat the caves."

"Why?" Stewart asked. "Do caves have feelings?"

"No, but there are rules. Remember what the ranger said, 'There are three main rules you need to follow while exploring any cave: Take nothing but pictures. Leave nothing but footprints. Kill nothing but time.' That pretty much covers it. We can't throw trash around inside, we aren't supposed to take anything out, and we have to leave the bugs and animals alone."

"What kind of things could a guy take from a cave anyway?" Jeff asked.

"Rocks, bugs, things like that. Oh, and we can't break off any of the stalactites or stalagmites."

"I always get those confused. Which is which?" Stewart groaned.

"It's easy," Hal answered. "Stalactites hold *tight* to the ceiling of the cave and stalagmites *might* reach up to the ceiling one day."

"Good, Hal. Mine is pretty simple too," Randy reported. "I've printed out a map for each of you that shows the location of all the known caves in the area, but the interesting part is how many there are. Some even have more than one entrance."

"How come?" Hal asked.

"This whole area is made up of limestone, fossils, and seashells from when water covered everything. After the mountains pushed up, it left great big holes in the ground, and there are a lot of those holes around here. Remember, one of the caves is called Endless Caverns."

"The thought of a cave that never ends gives me the shivers," Stewart said with a quivering voice. "Just think. We could go in and never find our way out."

"That's what I'm saying, Stewart. People can still find new

openings to caves because the process keeps going on even today."

"You mean new caves are popping up?" Stewart asked.

"Well, not new ones. I mean the ground keeps moving and the rain keeps coming down. That's why the formations in the caves still grow and why there can be new sinkholes that open into caves," Randy said.

"How do you know that?" Stewart asked.

"Well, because that's how Luray Caverns were first discovered. Some guys saw a new sinkhole, and it had cold air coming out. Rushing wind from the cave blew out the candle a man was holding while he was trying to make the hole bigger to see where it went."

"Man, I would love to be the one to discover a new entrance into a cave," Jeff wished. "You know, find a place that no one else knew about."

"I'll stick to the ones that have lights, handrails, and park rangers everywhere," Stewart declared.

Just then a voice on the scanner called,

"Adam 54 calling Base."

"Roger, 54."

"I'm 10-51."

"10-4."

"That sounds important," Hal said.

When Randy looked up 10-51, he sadly reported, "The guy's on a coffee break."

Stewart gave him a look that said, "Stewart is *very* upset."

"Stew, why don't you tell us what you've found out about the dangerous man-eating beasts that live in caves?"

"Funny, very funny. There are some critters we have to watch for. First, the best chance we have of running into animals is only near the place where we go in."

"How come?"

"That's because they don't like the dark and cold any more than I do. So as long as there is light, we might see raccoons, little rats, and stuff like that."

"What? No rattlesnakes, no mountain lions, no nothing?" Hal asked.

"It doesn't mean we don't have to be careful," Stewart sneered.

Randy agreed. "That's right, Stewart. What else did you find?"

"Well, also near the entrance there might be a whole bunch of things."

"Like what?"

"Let me see what I wrote down. Near the front we might find daddy longlegs, beetles, and salamanders. Way back in the dark you can find some creatures that are just plain weird."

"Now this is getting interesting," Jeff chuckled, rubbing his hands together.

"Some things living in the deepest part of a cave have never seen the light of day. In fact, they're completely blind."

"Cut it out," Jeff demanded.

"No, I'm serious. These things have no color on their little white bodies, and some of them don't have any eyes at all. But I've kept the worst for last," Stewart warned.

"What's that?" Hal questioned.

"Bats."

"Bats?" Randy asked. "What about bats?"

"Caves are lousy with bats. They hang upside down from the ceiling near the entrance. Then, at night they come out and eat bugs and stuff."

"I heard there are vampire bats that drink your blood," Jeff needled.

"Really?" Stewart asked as he shuffled quickly through his notes. "All I could find is they can't see anything. They're blind so they use a kind of radar to keep from splattering into trees or rocks. Bats *can* bite you, so we don't want to try and grab one."

"So what's the big problem?" Hal asked.

"It's what they leave on the floor of the cave after hanging around on the ceiling all day long."

"What?" they all asked.

"Let's just say that's why I suggested you might want to have some hip waders on," and he laughed. "Once we get past that part, the cave is supposed to be pretty clean."

"That should do it," Randy concluded. "Let's plan a special meeting back here on Friday after school. We can go over our checklists, fix up our helmet lights, and make sure we have everything we need. It'll give us a chance to fire up the ol' scanner again and just have it on in the background to see what's going on."

"Isn't there supposed to be a full moon on Friday?" Jeff asked

"So?" Stewart whimpered.

"Don't you know that the busiest time in a hospital emergency room is always on the night of a full moon?"

"It is?"

"Yup. That scanner should have smoke comin' out of it by Friday night."

Chapter 6

Randy sat with his family at the dinner table. Dinner included the predictable conversation about what happened at work, the activities at church, and how Randy was doing in school. He decided tonight was as good a time as any to get everything out.

He hadn't asked permission yet to spend Friday and Saturday night at Jeff's uncle's farm. They planned a campout and that wouldn't be a problem, but he needed to ask permission to use the hard hats too. He knew when his father heard that question he'd have a few more of his own.

"Are you doing anything interesting at school we should know about?" his mother questioned.

"The usual, but there is one thing. We have to do a report for science class."

"What are you reporting about?" she asked.

"Caves. Jeff, Hal, Stewart, and I decided to take four different cave subjects and then pool our information."

"Why would it matter who did what?" his father asked.

"Well, I need permission for a couple things."

"Fire away."

"First, we're planning to have a campout at the farm where Jeff's uncle lives. Would that be okay?"

"When are you thinking about doing this?" his mother wanted to know.

"This weekend."

Randy was known for telling the truth. Even at times when he knew he'd be punished after doing something wrong, he still admitted it and took his lumps. His father had often told him, "If you tell the truth, you don't have to wonder each time you tell your story. The truth will be the truth and that's it. When people tell a lie, they have to keep trying to remember what they told to whom. That's when they get into trouble."

"What about Sunday?" his mother asked.

"Oh, we can ride to church with Jeff's uncle. Besides, I wouldn't miss one of Mr. Roberts' classes unless I was in the hospital or something. I was wondering if I could use four of those hard hats you have out in the shed, Dad?"

"I don't mind if you use them, but what for?"

"We went to that cave information class the other day, remember?"

"Yes."

"Well, there's a cave entrance on the farm. We were sort of thinking about doing some exploring for the assignment, of course."

"Do the others have their parents' permission?" his mother

asked.

"They're supposed to be working on it."

"I don't know son. I'm in and out of caves around here all the time. A cave can be a very dangerous place, especially for beginners like you guys."

"I know. That's why our reports are about the caves in Virginia. We're researching safety, rules, and the animals that live there."

His mother cautioned, "Randy, I'm not so sure."

"We've been working really hard to get ready. You can look at my notes and my checklist if you want to."

"Well, son, as long as you let this uncle know where you are and when to expect you, and you promise not to go deep inside the cave without a guide, I don't see any problems."

"Thanks, Dad, I'm really excited about it."

Randy could tell his mother didn't want him to go, but she was like that about some things. His father was a different story. He often encouraged him to try new things, so he'd know what he wanted to do when he grew up.

Randy got on his computer later and instant-messaged the other three. "I got permission for the weekend. Let me know how you're doing."

One by one the others responded saying they could go. It seemed that Stewart had the most difficult time. His IM said, "My mother threatened to lock me in the house, but I told her I'd work extra hard on my science report and that this trip would guarantee me an A. That's all she needed to hear."

That made Randy laugh, but it was good. They could all go on the campout. It was going to take all four of them to come up with all the supplies they needed.

From that point, it seemed to Randy like the rest of the week was moving backward. *Why is it,* he wondered, *when you're doing something fun, the time goes way too fast? Then when you're waiting for something, time seems to stand still?*

The guys met in the lunchroom to go over their plans.

"Anyone having trouble getting the things we need?" Randy asked.

Item by item they worked their way down the list, but after only getting about halfay through, the bell rang.

"Aw nuts," Stewart complained. "I forgot to eat my lunch. Now I'm going to get a headache."

"Good. You already give the rest of us a headache anyway," Jeff nagged.

They agreed to meet again at lunch the next day. Randy hadn't expected it to take so long to get everything ready. He was beginning to wonder if they should postpone the trip for one more week, and he suggested that at lunch the next day.

"No way," Jeff argued. "We've been planning this long enough. I can hardly wait till this weekend as it is."

"Then we're just going to have to kick it up a notch. We need to make sure we have everything together by Thursday. That's the deadline."

"Thursday. Why Thursday?" Stewart questioned.

"Because. That will give us Friday night to do a final check. After that, it will be too late. My dad reminded me how dangerous caves can be, and I'm not taking any chances."

"I don't see why it's such a big deal," Jeff scoffed. "I mean we're only taking a look inside the opening of the cave, right?"

"That's right," Randy agreed, "but if this works out well, the next time we'll be prepared to take a look farther back."

"I don't like the sound of that," Stewart whimpered.

"Well, then you don't have to go the next time, Stewart," Jeff threatened.

"I'll be the one to decide if I go again or not. You won't."

"Yeah, right. It'll be your mommy who decides for you. Hey, I know. Why don't we bring her along?" Jeff teased.

"You leave my mother out of this."

"Gladly, Stewart, gladly," Jeff prodded.

Randy had heard just about enough bickering. "We don't need to go at all if you can't get along. Let's stop picking on each other and concentrate on what's important . . . getting in and out of that cave in one piece. We'll talk about food and water at lunch tomorrow."

"Ha. Do you make these things up on purpose?" Jeff asked.
"What?"

"Food and water, lunch, get it?"

Everybody started laughing including Randy.

It helped make the week go faster to have these daily

meetings. The boys were able to go over details at home each night and then come back to the next lunch session with more questions and ideas.

"That wraps it up," Randy announced. "We've covered everything. Don't feel stupid if you bring extra lights and food. Since this is our first cave, I don't mind if we overdo it for this one. Then the next time we'll feel better."

"I still plan to stick two lights on my helmet," Stewart insisted.

"Why don't you use three?" Jeff asked.

"Three? Why three?"

"You can put two regular ones on the front and a red one on the back. That way we'll know which way you're going."

"A license plate would look good too," Hal added.

"I'm warning you guys," Randy threatened. "Then it's settled," he added. "We'll meet in the shed tonight around six."

"What do we have left to do?" Jeff asked.

"It will take a long time to make sure our lights aren't going to fall off the hard hats. We need to pack our backpacks and do a final check."

"Check, check, check. All we do is check," Jeff complained. "I'm about ready to check out."

"That's up to you," Randy said.

"Hey, wait a minute. Don't forget I'm the guy with the farm that has the cave on it."

"How could we forget?" Stewart whined. "You remind us

every five minutes. I never saw anyone who was so proud of a dumb hole in the ground in my life."

"Tonight at six. Don't forget we'll be listening to the scanner."

"I remember," Stewart taunted. "With the full moon you guys promised me, there ought to be something to look forward to."

Chapter 7

By four-fifteen three bikes lay sprawled in Randy's backyard.

Rufus went out in the shed earlier with Randy, but when the others arrived, Rufus left.

"How come your dog doesn't stay around any more when we come over?" Stewart asked.

"I've always told you Rufus acts like he understands English. I think it has something to do with the first club meeting we had."

"Why? What happened?" Jeff asked.

"Don't you remember? We voted to make him our bomb-sniffing dog."

Rufus wasn't the brightest puppy in the litter. Randy always thought his dog was a few biscuits short of a full box, but every time the boys came over for their weekly meeting, Rufus ran recklessly off in the opposite direction. At least he had enough sense to know he didn't care to get close to anything that might blow him into next week.

Inside the shed the boys chattered like they always did. Randy already had the scanner on with the sound turned up full blast, but so far they only heard that annoying static.

Stewart looked over at the scanner. Then he looked up toward the ceiling of the shed and shouted, "Come on full moon don't let me down."

Everyone laughed. They continued packing their sleeping bags, backpacks, and supplies.

"Where are we going to sleep?" Hal asked.

"It isn't supposed to be very cold tonight, so I thought we could make a campsite out by the woods not too far from the cave. That way we can start exploring first thing in the morning," Jeff said.

Hal and Stewart started packing two ends of the same rope into their backpacks. It looked a little like a couple of people eating one strand of spaghetti at the same time. When they get to the middle, there was going to be trouble. Finally, Hal gave one last tug on the rope and the other half of it started coming out of Stewart's bag.

"Hey," Stewart complained, as only Stewart knew how, "what do you think you're doing?"

They looked at the rope both were trying to pack and started laughing.

"It's a good thing we aren't getting ready to go sky diving," Randy joked. "I wouldn't want you two anywhere *near* my parachute."

"Hurry up you guys," Jeff insisted. "My dad's going to be here any minute with his truck to take us to the farm. You'd better be ready or we'll have to leave without you."

"Don't tempt me," Stewart shot back.

They were down to just a few more things to pack. Randy tried to make sure everyone had equal weight to carry. Then he said, "There isn't anything happening around here, so I'm going to switch to the state police channel. I looked it up last night."

"So much for our full moon," Stewart grumbled.

The static pattern changed a little after Randy tuned in the state police. It seemed like nothing was going to happen there either. But then, all of a sudden, they heard it.

First, there were several sounds like an alert of some kind. All four sets of eyes turned immediately to that sound.

"What was that?" Stewart asked.

"Shhh!" the others went at the same time.

"Dispatcher here. Adam 52, Adam 53. 10-93, alarm at Dominion State Bank."

"Adam 52. 10-4."

"Adam 53. 10-4."

"Dispatcher to Sam 20, did you copy the traffic on the alarm?"

"Sam 20. 10-4, I'm 10-35 now."

At that moment four mouths dropped open at the Hilton Park Road Detective Club.

"I don't think I like this," Stewart growled.

"Like it? I *love* it!" Jeff screamed.

"Dispatcher to Adam 52 and 53."

"Adam 52. 10-4."

"Adam 53. 10-4."

Then the alert tone sounded again like before.

"Dispatcher to all units, valid alarm. Suspects left west bound from the bank lot in a blue, older model sedan. No plate information. Two white males with ski masks and armed with shotguns. Suspect number one, 5'10", medium build, wearing blue pants and black shirt. Suspect number two, 6'2", slender, wearing white shirt and jeans."

"Wow!" Hal said in a whisper.

"You said it," Randy answered.

"Adam 53. 10-23 will get further."

"Dispatcher. Copy, 52?"

"Adam 52. 10-4."

"Dispatcher. FBI and King 16 will be in route."

"Guys," Jeff exclaimed, "this is big! I'm telling you really big!"

"Adam 52. 10-35."

"It all happened so fast I didn't have a chance to give you the police radio codes I printed for you guys. But one thing I heard doesn't need any code. She said the FBI," Randy gasped in a trembling voice, "The FBI!"

"Adam 53 to station."

"Dispatcher. Go ahead Adam 53."

"Adam 53. I've got a 10-57 blue sedan over here at 19ᵗʰ Street West and Jefferson. Doors are open, no suspects."

Another tone came screaming over the scanner.

"Dispatcher. All units are advised suspects have abandoned vehicle. Alert all jurisdictions, suspects are in another vehicle headed for the Interstate."

"They got away?" Stewart asked. "They got away," he whispered the answer to his own question.

"That means they could be anywhere," Randy said.

"Yeah, and I don't think it's such a great idea for us to be sleeping out in the dark on a farm someplace with bank robbers on the loose," Stewart grumbled.

"That's stupid," Jeff said. "My uncle's farm is in the middle of nowhere."

"My point exactly," Stewart said, folding his arms in defiance.

"By morning they'll probably be a thousand miles away from this place," Jeff assured.

Just then they heard the loud roar of an engine as someone pulled up outside the shed. Stewart ran to a corner and hid behind some boxes.

"What is *wrong* with you?" Jeff asked. "You're shaking like a paint can in a hardware store's mixing machine."

"It's the robbers. I know it is," Stewart wailed. "You heard it. They've got shotguns."

"So what?" Hal demanded.

"You don't even have to aim a shot gun. When one of those things goes off, it can hit everything in sight," Stewart sputtered.

The door to the shed slowly opened. The grinding of the old rusty hinges only added to Stewart's worries. All eyes were glued to those worn, weathered boards. All eyes, that is except Stewart's. His were closed so tight it would take dynamite to get them open.

Chapter 8

"You guys ready to go yet?" a voice called out.

"No! I'm too young to die!" Stewart cried.

"It's only Jeff's dad," Randy sighed with relief. "Come on out, Stewart."

They quickly loaded everything in back of the truck and were finally on their way. No one said a word about the bank robbery. They wanted to make sure they could still go on the campout. Randy reminded them if it hadn't been for the scanner, they wouldn't know about it either.

The farm where they were going was only about ten miles away. The truck turned down a long, dirt lane with rusty fences on both sides held up by jagged, old wooden posts. Gnarled vines grew over these barricades forming thick tall hedges. The truck stopped at the edge of the woods, and the boys tossed their things in a big pile. Jeff's dad drove away, and it was time to set up camp.

"I don't like sleeping out tonight," Stewart complained. "Those robbers could be near us right now."

"Look," Jeff thundered, "we aren't going to sit around all night and listen to you complain. I picked out a great place to camp where no one could ever see us even if they did come back here."

He led them to a place where several large fallen logs had been stacked. It looked almost like an old frontier fort.

"We can put our sleeping bags behind these logs and stay out of sight. Is that okay with you, Stewart?"

"I guess so, but I still don't like it."

For the next couple of hours they enjoyed a campfire and then settled in for the night.

"You guys want me to tell a scary story?" Jeff asked.

"Don't you dare," Stewart pleaded.

Jeff was the storyteller of the group. Whenever they had a campout, he always tried his best to scare the wits out of everyone.

In a low, spooky voice, he began his tale. "This is a story I call *The Alligator in the Lake.*"

"Can't be too scary," Hal said. "We aren't anywhere near a lake out here."

"A man in Florida called a detective agency because he'd been having problems with an alligator."

"I think I'm going to like this one," Randy said. "It has detectives in it."

"Of course they're going to have trouble with alligators," Stewart criticized. "Everybody has problems with alligators in Florida. That's where alligators live. Didn't the man know that?"

In a hushed and quivering voice Jeff continued. "But this is different."

"You mean his alligators were a different color or something?" Stewart mocked.

Jeff went on, "The man said, 'My problems are different than anything that I have ever heard of before, and I've lived in Florida for a long, long time.'"

Stewart asked, "Problems? What kind of problems?"

"The man told them, 'One day, old Fred who lives farther up the lake, was out fishing minding his own business. When he turned around to get some fresh bait for his hook, he looked and all his bait was gone.'"

Hal laughed and suggested, "Maybe the fish were really biting that day."

"Let me tell you something else," Jeff added. "The Martins who lived just down the street were having a picnic in their backyard and close by the lake. They set their food down just for a couple minutes to play catch, but when they came back, their lunch was gone!"

Stewart didn't know what to say. This was unusual for Stewart because he was almost never at a loss for words.

"Then the man told them, 'But that's not the worst of it.'"

Stewart asked, "You mean it gets worse than your bait's missing and losing your lunch? I didn't think there could be anything worse than losing your lunch."

"'Yes,' replied the man," Jeff said.

"What could be worse?" Hal asked.

"The man told the detective, 'The Petersons came to visit their Uncle Jeb. They let their dog, their tiny fluffy innocent little puppy-dog, play out in the backyard by the lake. All of a sudden, *he* was missing!'"

In a whispering voice, Stewart asked, "What do you mean, he was missing?"

"The Petersons found his collar in the grass. There were a couple of clawing marks in the sand on the beach, but the puppy was *gone!*" Jeff cried.

"That's terrible," Stewart exclaimed.

"Then the detectives decided to get right on the case. They planned to conduct their investigation at night since using flashlights is the easiest way to see alligators. The detectives went down to a hardware store and bought two flashlights, extra batteries, and a set of walkie-talkies so they could talk to each other."

"Flashlights like we got, huh?" Randy asked.

"Next, they decided on a plan. One was going to hide behind a tree, and the other would walk along the beach to see what might happen. They waited until it got dark. They waited. And they waited. And then they waited some more."

"I don't think I'm going to like this," Stewart groaned. "Even if it turns out good, I already don't like it."

"When it was about midnight, one of the detectives shined his flashlight out into the water, and he thought he saw something.

But it disappeared. The second detective shined his light out from where he was hiding, and he *did* see something."

"What?" Stewart asked.

"What he saw was just above the surface of the water."

"What? What did he see?"

"Two creepy, red eyes, glowing like hot coals from a fire were moving straight toward the first detective."

"Ohhhh," Stewart groaned.

"As you can imagine, he was really pretty scared by this time. But he had a net to catch the alligator, and the second detective had a rope. Those eerie, red eyes came closer and closer, closer and closer."

"What, what, what?" Stewart demanded.

"The first detective jumped out with his net and threw it over the alligator's head while the second one took his rope and tied it around the tail. They yanked that alligator right out of the water and onto the beach."

"What were they going to do with it now?" Hal asked.

"They hadn't really thought about that part yet. They dragged it up farther on the beach, and guess what happened?"

"What?" Stewart asked in a hoarse voice.

"Batteries fell out."

"*Batteries?*" Hal asked.

"Right out of its stomach," Jeff said. "Have you ever heard of an alligator with batteries in its stomach?"

"No," the rest of the boys said all at once.

"Well, that's what this one had. It had batteries."

"I don't get it," Stewart said.

"It must have eaten Stewart's backpack 'cause it's full of batteries," Hal laughed.

"No, this was a radio-controlled alligator. Do you know why it was in that water?"

"No!" They all questioned again, "Why?"

"There was a man who wanted to build houses by that lake, and he was trying to scare everyone away so they wouldn't want to live there. If the people moved away, he would be able to control all of the land that he wanted, and he could make millions of dollars."

Stuart protested, "What a rotten trick."

"The detectives used their special radio scanner to find the transmitter that had been sending signals to operate that alligator."

"Kind of like the scanner we have," Randy said.

"All they had to do was follow that signal right back to the man who owned it, and that's exactly what they did. They found him on the other side of the lake in an electronic control room filled with video monitors, radios, and a map of the entire lake."

"Wish your shed was like that, Randy," Hal said.

"The private detectives called the police, and the man was arrested. He went to court the next week to go on trial."

"What happened?" the guys asked at almost the same time.

"They found him guilty. Now, instead of sending him to

prison for such an evil crime, do you know what the judge did?"

"Of course, we don't," Stewart complained. "Why don't you tell us?"

"Instead of sending him to jail, the judge sent the criminal to work in a zoo. For the next few years, he was sentenced to feed all the crocodiles, alligators, and snakes."

"The detectives became big heroes, and the man who had hired them decided he would build some houses himself. Then he gave each detective a house he could use for the rest of his life, so that anytime he wanted to come to Florida he could stay in his own place right on the lake."

"That's why I want to be a detective," Hal said, "so when I solve crimes, people will give me stuff."

"That's no reason," Randy objected. "Just stopping criminals should be enough. The detectives probably never expected to get such a nice place on a lake."

"Speaking of the lake," Jeff concluded, "if I were you, I wouldn't go out there in the dark at around midnight with a flashlight. You never know if there really might be an alligator there."

Randy always enjoyed Jeff's stories. "Hey, thanks, Jeff, that was one of your best."

"How do you come up with them anyway?" Hal asked. "They're just as good as the cartoons on TV."

"Thank you, thank you," Jeff boasted as he took a bow. "They just come to me. Now how about another one? Let me see.

Should I tell a scary cave story or one about the thing that came out of the woods?"

"No more stories," Stewart begged. "Please."

"We need to get to sleep," Randy said. "Tomorrow is going to be a big day."

"I just have one more question, Jeff," Hal said. "Why do they call it Abbott's Cave? Your name isn't Abbott, and neither is your uncle's."

"All I've ever heard is over a hundred years ago some guy named Dr. Abbott went in to explore the cave, and he never came out."

"Oh man," Stewart whined, "I *really* didn't need to hear that."

"They named it after him," Jeff added.

"I wonder if there's a big hole in there." Hal said.

It was a clear night. There wasn't even a breeze. Every star in the sky looked like it had been cleaned and polished just for them. Randy especially noticed the full moon. It lit up the campsite like a giant night light.

He heard an owl way off in the distance. Randy noticed that Stewart didn't seem to like the owl at all. Then there was a rustling sound in the leaves not far from where they were lying on the ground.

"What was that?" Stewart asked.

"Go to sleep," Hal told him.

Randy watched as Stewart slowly slid like a salamander

until he was as far down into his sleeping bag as he could get.

"Good night, Stewart," Randy comforted.

"There's nothing *good* about it."

The night was quiet. It was peaceful, and they were away from the rest of the world. It didn't take long until everyone was asleep and their small fire went out.

A few hours later Randy thought he was dreaming. It sounded like a car was slowly coming down the same dirt road they had driven in on, but he couldn't see any lights. He looked at his watch. It was only four-thirty in the morning.

Suddenly the sound stopped. Randy looked around but he couldn't see anything.

Then he heard a car door shut, and then a second. When the second door closed, all four boys were sitting straight up in their sleeping bags.

"What's that noise?" Stewart asked.

Randy slipped out of his sleeping bag and peeked over the top of a big log. In the moonlight he could see two men standing at the back of a car. One man was short and fat. The other one was tall and thin. They each wore dark clothes and black ski hats. Neither man said a word.

They each had a flashlight and the short man opened the trunk. He pulled out a large, dark duffel bag and set it on the ground. The thin man reached into the trunk and took out two long shiny things.

"Shotguns," Randy whispered.

"Where?" Stewart asked.

"Be *quiet*," Randy told him.

Now the other three joined Randy behind the log.

The men closed the trunk and quickly disappeared into the woods. The boys watched until they couldn't see the light from the flashlights anymore.

"Are those the robbers?" Stewart asked.

"Stewart, sometimes I really wonder about you," Jeff said. "Of course it's them."

The boys sat there, stunned.

For the next several minutes they whispered about what they should do.

Suddenly Hal said, "I think they're coming back."

In silence the boys watched as the two men returned to their car.

"Hey, they ditched their flashlights. Must be because the moon is so bright," Jeff noted.

"They don't have the bag or the guns either," Randy added.

The men climbed back into their car, started the engine, and began to turn around in the tall grass.

"We should have done something so their car wouldn't start," Jeff said.

"I'm too scared to move," Stewart whimpered.

They watched helplessly as the car slipped slowly back down the lane with its lights off. Then it was gone.

"We should do something," Hal said.

"Like what?" Stewart asked.

"I don't know. Anything."

"It should be light soon," Randy told them. "I think we can take a quick look around the cave in the morning, and then we'd better tell someone."

"They must have hidden the money out there in the woods someplace," Jeff said.

"Oh great," Stewart added. "That's all I needed to hear."

"Soon as the sun comes up, let's eat breakfast, mess around in the cave entrance for a few minutes, and then we'd better tell your uncle what we saw, Jeff," Randy suggested.

Everyone agreed.

"I wouldn't mind having that scanner right about now so we knew what's going on," Stewart said.

"We can check out the cave. Then that will be it," Randy repeated.

"We'll be in and out in no time. I mean what could possibly happen, right?" Hal added.

Chapter 9

Spying those two dark figures was one of the most terrifying sights any of the boys had ever witnessed. The men made Jeff's alligator story look silly by comparison. The boys slid back into the safety of their sleeping bags but one thing was sure. No one went back to sleep.

All they could do was lie there with their eyes wide open. Randy peered over at Stewart in the moonlight, and it looked like he was trying not to blink if he didn't have to so his eyes wouldn't close. Randy tried closing his eyes a couple of times, but all he could see in his mind were the two men and those shotguns. He hoped they were anything except criminals.

The next hour and a half seemed like days, and then, finally, they could hear birds singing in the trees. First, one bird, then another, and yet another sang out until the air was alive with beautiful chirping sounds of all kinds. They were a comfort to Randy but only slightly.

Soon the sky began to brighten. As the sun came up, Randy and the others tried to put out of their minds what they had seen.

It was as if no one said anything about it, then maybe it never really happened.

The boys quietly packed up their things and ate breakfast. By this time the sun was fully up and the air was getting warmer. They stacked the things that weren't needed for the cave in a pile and covered them with branches. With their backpacks and hard hats, the four explorers set off to locate the cave's entrance.

"None of the rest of us has seen your cave before, Jeff," Randy mentioned. "You'd better lead the way."

"I've only been here once myself. My uncle showed me where it was, but I've never gone inside. I only saw the opening."

"So you don't know if it's big or small or anything?" Hal asked.

"Nope. I think it's over this way," Jeff said with confidence.

After they had walked only a few more steps, Stewart stopped dead in his tracks. "Hey, isn't this the same way those two guys went last night?"

"We don't know exactly *where* they went," Randy answered.

"Nobody knows about this cave," Jeff reminded them. "It's on private property and no one is allowed to come out this way except for me because it's my uncle's. He only lets family come back here."

"Oh, right . . . family," Stewart responded defiantly. "So I suppose Dumb and Not So Smart out here last night were just a couple of your long lost cousins."

"I'm not saying people don't wander around out here

sometimes, but it would be almost impossible to find the cave if you didn't know where it was."

"Your uncle found it. Didn't he?" Stewart asked sarcastically.

Jeff turned and went into some thicker brush. "This way, I think," he indicated, and the rest followed close behind.

"Are you sure there's a cave out here?" Hal asked.

"Yeah, my backpack is really getting heavy," Stewart complained.

"It wouldn't if you hadn't filled it up with batteries. Those things are heavy," Jeff countered.

"Tell me about it."

They walked on for another few minutes. It was difficult because of the load they carried, and the ground threatened them with jagged rocks and thick brush. Branches hung down from towering trees all around making it a slow hike for everyone.

Trudging on, they came to one very large branch that Jeff had to push back from the trail. As each boy passed by he handed the branch off to the next. That is until Stewart came along. Thinking Stewart would grab it, Randy let the branch go, but at that moment, Stewart was adjusting the straps on his backpack again. The branch flew out of Randy's hand and hit Stewart right in the chest. It knocked him flat on his back. He struggled but couldn't get back up.

"Hey, you guys," he whined.

Jeff turned around and started laughing. "Man, you look

like a turtle that can't turn back over."

"It's not funny. Somebody help me get up."

They all helped Stewart get back on his feet and then walked around the other side of the tree.

"We should be pretty close I think," Jeff assured. Then, as they made their way to the top of a small ridge, he exclaimed triumphantly, "There it is!"

Quickly the rest of the guys scrambled up to see for themselves.

"I was expecting a big opening like at Mammoth Cave," Randy said, slightly disappointed.

"Wait a minute," Hal said. "What's that?"

"What?" Stewart shouted.

"That." Hal pointed to some crumpled papers near the cave entrance.

The boys moved toward the papers to get a closer look. Randy got there first and picked them up.

"What are they?" Jeff asked.

"I'm not sure, but this one has the word Dominion written on it."

Hal took one of the others out of Randy's hand. "This one is some kind of diagram. Look."

"I think we should get out of here," Stewart warned. "That cave isn't going anyplace. We can come back here anytime."

"What do you think, Randy?" Jeff asked.

"We've worked pretty hard to get ready for this trip, and

we're standing right in front of the cave now. I think we should at least have a look. Tell you what, let's vote on it like we do back at the shed when we have to decide important stuff."

There wasn't any other suggestion so Randy said, "All in favor raise your hand."

The vote was three to one.

"Stewart!" Jeff demanded.

Stewart slowly raised his hand.

"That makes it unanimous," Randy announced.

"Not really," Stewart mumbled.

"I'll put these papers in my backpack. We're a detective club so they'll be evidence."

"That's a good idea," Hal added.

Then Randy gave the order, "Before we go in we must check out our lights and stuff to make sure we have everything."

They sat on a couple fallen logs and took off their backpacks.

"Oh, that feels so good," Stewart grunted as he let his fall. "I thought I was going to die. I really don't know why we're doing this," he complained, "if we're just going to take a look inside. We ought to leave all this junk out here. We'd save time, and we could get back out sooner to tell on those guys we saw."

"Rules are rules, Stewart. We have to do this by the book. That's what the ranger said. Don't you remember *anything* from that class?" Randy said.

"I remember plenty, and I also remember I'd like to see the sun come up a few more times. If those goons come back while we're out here, I might not get to do that."

"They're probably clear in another state by now," Jeff added. "Even if they did hide the money out here someplace on my uncle's farm, I don't think they'll be coming back for it until things cool down."

"Jeff's right. I don't think we have anything to worry about," Hal confirmed.

"Let's go then," Randy ordered.

They struggled to get their packs back on, made sure they hadn't dropped anything, and set out for the final short climb to the cave's entrance. Jeff continued to lead. The path was so narrow the boys had to walk in single file. They looked like a pack of broken-down mules lumbering up a narrow pass in the Colorado mountains. Jeff reached the entrance first.

"Hey, come up here. You can feel cold air coming out."

"What do you think is the best way for us to go in?" Randy asked Jeff.

"I think we should get down and crabwalk like we do in gym class relays."

The entrance to the cave had wet rocks. Several of them were a little slippery. With all that weight on their backs it would be easy to take a pretty nasty fall. Doing the crabwalk turned out to be a good idea.

The entrance was about the size of a car door. Only one person would be able to wiggle in at a time.

"Who wants to go first?" Randy asked.

"I will," Jeff volunteered. "I think we'll have to take our packs off again. We can crawl in and then pull the packs in after us."

"Take off your hard hat too," Hal urged. "You don't want to break your light on the top of the entrance."

"Yeah, but don't break your head on the way in either," Randy cautioned.

"I won't."

"Here, take a flashlight so you can see where to put your feet," Randy said.

Jeff peered into the opening. He put his head inside then decided to turn around and go in feet first. He reached back out and dragged his backpack through the hole. Then he was gone.

"Oh my goodness!" a voice yelled from inside the cave. "You guys are *not* gonna believe this place. Hurry up and come on in."

One by one they slithered through the opening. It took a few seconds for Randy's eyes to adjust to the light. "Hey, it's like the ranger said. There's enough light from the entrance to see just a little way into the cave."

"Now I see why they make such a big deal about bringing your own lights," Hal said.

"And a *lot* of them too," Stewart reminded everyone.

"Let's get our backpacks and hard hats on, so we can do some serious exploring," Jeff said.

It wasn't long before they had completely forgotten about the men they had seen. The wonder that appeared as they shined their lights was all the explorers could think about at the moment.

"How come we can't see any stalagmites or stalactites?" Stewart asked.

"That's because we're staying too *tight* to the entrance, and we *might* see some if we go farther back in the cave," Jeff joked.

"Hey, look up there you guys. What's that?"

"What, *what?*" Stewart asked with his usual alarm.

"Up there. Those."

As they began to look up toward the ceiling of the cave, the lights on their hard hats aimed up there too. The ceiling shimmered like grain in a wheat field on a windy day.

"Those are *bats*," Randy said.

"Oh no, not bats!" Stewart wailed. "I really *hate* bats."

"Big surprise, Stewart, big surprise," Jeff laughed.

Then Stewart looked down toward his feet, and the light on his hat went down there too. "Guys, hey guys," he said in a quivering voice.

"What?" they all asked.

"Take a look at your feet."

Randy took one look at what was going on down there and said, "I'm really glad they told us to wear good boots." He could see what the bats had left behind after years and years of hanging around up there, but that was only part of it. A teaming mass of salamanders, spiders, beetles, and other insects scurried in all directions.

"Sometimes a guy can have too much light," Stewart said

with a shiver.

"This is like something out of a movie," Jeff said.

"I think if we go in where it's a little darker we can get away from the bat hangout. It should be cleaner in there too," Randy suggested.

"I wonder if soldiers used this cave as a hideout during the Civil War," Hal said.

"I read they did use caves to get some of the chemicals to make gun powder, but who knows? This opening might not have been here then," Randy reminded them. "Keep your lights on and step carefully. We don't want someone falling in a hole or anything."

"Are there holes like that in here?" Stewart asked.

"There could be. Just be careful, that's all," Randy said.

"Don't forget good ol' Doctor Abbott," Jeff warned.

As they cautiously moved around the sharp edge of a large rock that jutted out into their path, Stewart hit something hard with both feet. He tripped and went sprawling onto the cave floor.

"Stewart, I said be careful. Are you okay?" Randy asked.

"I think so. Only I tripped over something."

"No kidding," Jeff laughed.

"No, really you guys. There's something down here."

"I thought caves weren't supposed to have any big animals," Hal said.

Again they aimed their lights in the direction where Stewart had fallen. Every one saw it at the same instant. There was no mistake now. All the events of the last night came flooding back.

"I wish we hadn't come in here," Stewart moaned.

Chapter 10

Stewart looked down near his feet where a large duffel bag rested on its side.

"Is that what I think it is?" Jeff asked.

Randy didn't say anything.

"What are we going to do?" Hal asked.

"I don't know about the rest of you guys," Jeff answered, "but I say we open it."

Quickly they dropped to their knees around where Stewart was still crumpled in a heap on the cave floor. Jeff dragged the bag closer.

"Man, this thing is really heavy."

He turned it upright again so the zipper was in plain view.

"Well, what are you waiting for?" Stewart asked.

Cautiously Jeff began to tug at the leather tab connected to the bag's zipper.

"Careful," Hal warned. "That thing could be booby-trapped."

Jeff stopped what he was doing and turned to Hal, "Did you have to say that?"

"Well, it could be."

Then Randy spoke up, "Those guys didn't expect anyone to find it. I doubt they did anything except stash it in here while they went out to see if they'd get stopped by the police."

But Stewart added, "For all we know they could be on their way back here right this minute."

"Stewart!" they all groaned.

"Go ahead," Randy gestured. "Open it." He aimed a beam of light at the bag.

Jeff grabbed the leather tab and slid the zipper open to reveal stacks and stacks of money. It was more money than any of them had ever seen in their lives.

Jeff laughed. "Is this your mother's purse, Stewart?"

"There must be a million dollars in there," Hal figured.

"Two million for sure," Jeff added.

Stewart thought for a minute and then squealed, "Two million dollars. I'm going to be so rich my mom will have to ask *me* for money from now on." They all laughed. Their echo could be heard deep into the cave.

"Be serious," Randy said. "We don't get to keep any of this money."

"What do you mean?" Jeff asked. "Finder keepers, remember?"

"Not with bank robbery money. It belongs to the bank they stole it from, and the money needs to go back there."

"Sometimes I hate being honest," Stewart complained, "and

this is one of those times. I really hate it."

Their eyes stayed fixed on the mountain of cash that filled the bag to over flowing.

Then Hal noticed something. "Hey, look! They left their flashlights and shotgun shells in the bag too."

"What was that?" Stewart asked in his usual disaster alarm voice.

"That's not funny," Randy scolded.

"No, I *mean* it. I heard something."

"You're always hearing things," Hal reminded. "Except for the bats, we're the only ones in here."

"Wait. I just heard something too," Jeff whispered.

"Maybe it's your uncle."

The area where Stewart tripped over the bag lay inside the darkened area of the cave just a few feet beyond the reach of light from the entrance.

"Quick," Randy ordered, "switch off all your lights."

"I'm not turning off my lights," Stewart protested.

"Turn them off or I'll do it for you," Jeff threatened.

Reluctantly, Stewart turned off the lights on his hard hat, plunging the boys into total darkness.

"It's darker in here than our Sunday school class ever was," Randy whispered.

"I'd give anything to be back there right this minute," Hal added. "Whatta we do now, Randy?"

"I saw a rocky ridge just behind us before we turned off our lights. Let's drag the bag back there, so I can think for a minute."

They hurried to pull the heavy duffel bag farther into the cave. Randy pulled a smaller flashlight out of his backpack so they weren't blindly going into even greater danger. The rocks jutted out from the cave floor far enough so they were able to crouch down behind them.

From this new vantage point the boys could see a little bit of the cave entrance. As his eyes adjusted, Randy could faintly make out the forms of two men coming through it. One man was short and heavy. The other was taller and very thin. The big man seemed to be in charge because he told the thin man what to do.

"I don't think they brought any lights," Randy said in a hushed voice.

"So what are we going to do?" Stewart asked.

"Do?" Jeff whispered. "We *do* nothing."

"That's right," Randy added. "If we stay quiet they might think someone else came in here, found their money, and took it."

"This is *not* gonna be pretty," Stewart cautioned. He was right. The men slowly crept over to where they had stowed the bag of money only to discover that it was gone.

The large man yelled, "You lousy thief, you stole it."

"Who you calling a thief? We're both thieves, remember?"

"Oh, yeah."

"Besides, I haven't been out of your sight since we brung it in here last night."

"Then suppose you tell me where our money went."

Waving his arms wildly in the air the thin man shouted, "We left it right here. I remember because it was next to the shotguns, and those are still here."

"Yeah, big deal. We unloaded them and left all the shells in the bag, and it ain't here, remember?"

"It was your brilliant plan to leave the flashlights in there too."

Their voices made a strange booming echo bouncing all over the cave's hard surfaces.

"I have a very bad feeling about this," the short man groaned.

"Can you believe someone would come into this cave, find our money, and steal it from us? You just can't trust nobody these days."

With a whisper Randy reminded his friends, "We have plenty of food and water, and we all wore warm clothes. It's a good thing we went to that class. In fact, we could stay in here for days if we had to."

"Days?" Stewart whispered.

"I think they'll get mad and leave. When they do, we'll wait till it's safe, and then we can get out of here."

"I'm all for that," Jeff said.

"Me too," Hal whispered.

The two robbers continued to argue about who was the bigger dummy. Randy thought that was a toss-up.

Then the heavy, short one decided, "We're going to have to

take our guns and rob another bank. That's all there is to it."

"I don't think I like the sound of that," the second complained, "Besides that we don't have any shells, remember?"

"Hey, Stewart, is that one of your relatives? He complains just like you."

Stewart didn't say anything, and if the boys had been out in the light, everyone could have seen why.

The men took their shotguns and turned to go back out the cave entrance when all of a sudden the unthinkable happened.

Stewart suddenly sneezed.

He let out the most powerful blast any of the boys had ever heard. The echo was so loud Randy thought it sounded like a hundred other Stewarts were in the cave with them.

Instantly, the men spun around in the direction where the boys were hiding.

"Who's in here?" one of them demanded in a booming voice.

"Just us cave rats," Stewart sniffed.

"Oh," the thin man said.

"Wait a minute," the first man stammered.

"We know you're there," yelled the second man. "You'd better not have our money."

"What kind of a stupid thing is that to say? They sure *better* have it."

"Now you've done it, Stewart," Jeff warned.

"I couldn't help it. It's cold in here."

The men moved toward where the boys were hiding. It was

too dark for them to see anything, but they were coming closer and closer.

"We have to get out of here," Randy warned. "Let's start crawling on our hands and knees. Each person's gotta hold on to the guy's jacket in front of you. But whatever you do, don't turn on any lights. Now, let's get moving," he whispered.

Randy took the lead, and at that moment he felt thankful Mr. Roberts had taught them about what to do if you lose one of your senses. He began to carefully feel the cave floor with his hands. He listened to see if there were any dangers ahead. He couldn't describe it, but somehow he was able to sense it when he came close to the wall or a big rock. Suddenly, he stopped and the rest of the boys all crammed together in a heap like a chain reaction accident.

"I have an idea," Randy whispered. "These guys don't sound like they graduated at the top of their bank robber class. We might be able to get them to follow us farther into the dark. Then they'll be stranded in here, and we can wait till help comes."

"What help?" Hal asked.

"You all told your parents we'd be in here, didn't you?"

"I didn't," Stewart admitted. "My mom would never have let me come."

"I didn't either," Hal added. "My parents think we're just camping."

"Jeff, you asked your uncle, right?"

"Uh, no."

"That's perfect," Randy said with a sigh. "You mean *nobody* knows we're in here?"

"Those two guys know," Stewart said.

"Didn't you tell your parents, Randy?" Hal asked.

"Yes, I did, but my dad could never find this place. Besides, they don't expect to see us again until we show up for church tomorrow."

"We might have to sleep in here," Jeff said.

"Who could sleep?"

"Quiet, Stewart."

The men were getting closer now. Surrounded by pitch black darkness, Randy knew they had to go deeper into the cave.

"Follow me, guys. I have a plan."

"Oh, I was hoping you would say something like that," Stewart said hopefully.

Like four blind mice the boys ventured deeper and deeper into the cave unable to see the dangers that might be lurking just around the next corner.

Chapter 11

When Randy calculated they might be far enough away from the two men, he stopped again. "Okay, we can stand up now, but feel around first to make sure you don't hit your head on anything."

Quietly they stood to their feet. Randy reached up above his head and felt nothing but air. "I'm going to give out two commands, and you have to follow them exactly. Every time I say 'on' you turn on your light, and when I say 'off', turn it off right away."

"Won't they be able to catch us when they see our lights?" Hal asked.

"That's what I want them to think. Each time we turn our lights on we can walk safely a few more steps, and each time we do that those guys will come deeper into the darkness."

"I'm scared," Stewart whispered.

"We all are. Now follow me." Randy walked a few more steps and commanded, "On."

The boys reached up to their hard hats and turned on the

flashlights. Stewart turned on both of his. Randy quickly glanced around to see if they could walk farther.

"Hey, there they are!" one of the men hollered. "Let's get'em!"

They rushed toward the boys when suddenly Randy called out, "Off!"

All at once the lights went out except for Stewart's. It took him longer to turn off the second one.

"Only use one next time, Stewart."

In the darkness the men were lost. "Ow! I just hit my head," the thin one cried. "That's going to make a big bump."

"You're going to have more than a bump to worry about if we don't catch them kids."

After moving several more steps, Randy again said, "On."

Just like rats trying to find the cheese at the end of a maze, the crooks kept coming.

"Off," Randy ordered.

Again everything went dark.

The boys inched their way along keeping close to the wall and shuffling their feet to help feel their way. Randy thought the worst thing that could happen to them had happened. Stewart had given away their hiding place with his bombastic sneeze. If it hadn't been for that noise, the robbers would be gone by now. *Then we'd be safe*, he thought. But was he ever wrong!

Each time the boys turned their lights on and off the distance between them and the crooks widened.

Again Randy ordered that the lights be turned on and then off. The men came deeper and deeper into the cave toward the boys. Somehow in the confusion of the darkness Stewart found himself in the lead. It would be too dangerous for Randy to try to fix that now. The crooks weren't far enough away.

"Keep moving," he whispered.

"Hey," one of the men said, "I think I feel something warm."

"Of course you do. You've got your hands on my face."

"Oh, sorry boss."

By the sound of their voices Randy could tell they were far enough away that it was safe to turn their lights on again.

"On."

The boys switched on their helmet lights, and once again the crooks came a little closer. Then Stewart tilted his head to look down where he was standing. The sight of what he saw next made him scream. As long as the guys had known him and with a lifetime of complaining, they had never heard him make a sound like that before.

"Looooook!" he exclaimed. They all looked down just in time to see a huge, black hole in the floor that stretched across the entire path, blocking their escape.

"Now what?" Hal asked in desperation.

Just then Stewart aimed his head down so far his hard hat came off. He frantically fumbled for it, but it was no use. The boys watched helplessly as it began a seemingly endless drop. The helmet hit one side of the shaft so hard that the burning flashlight came loose and sailed all the way across to the other side. When it hit that wall, the light shattered extinguishing its precious beam. The boys listened, and listened, and listened. In what seemed like an eternity, they finally heard the hard hat crash to the bottom.

"I'm glad my head isn't still in that thing."

While all of this was happening, the boys totally forgot about the two men who were almost on top of them. The first one tripped and fell causing the second man to stumble over him, and he fell right on top of his partner. In the darkness it was difficult for them to get untangled.

With his small flashlight, Randy looked down next to the wall and noticed a small rock shelf in the floor about the size of a window ledge. It went all the way around one side of the hole.

"Stewart!" he yelled. "Start walking on that ledge."

"Over my dead body."

"Okay, if we have to," Jeff threatened. "Now move it."

Stewart was frozen in his position. "This is just great. I'm scared of the dark, I'm absolutely terrified of heights, and right now I got both."

Even though he tried, he couldn't move his feet, not even an inch.

"Come on, Stewart," Hal complained, "try to think of it as depths. You aren't afraid of depths are you?"

"I don't know. That's a new one."

The crooks finally got free from each other on the floor and began to get back on their feet.

"Those guys are going to throw all of us down there where your stuff went if you don't get going."

"I can't, honest. I really can't."

"Just stare at the wall," Randy pleaded. "You don't have to look down."

"Don't worry. That's the *last* place I want to look."

"As long as you keep your toes against the wall you can ease your feet along the ledge. Come on, man. We're all depending on you."

Randy couldn't remember ever depending on Stewart for anything except a complaint. Now he meant everything to them.

"We need you."

Hal gave Stewart a gentle nudge, and he began moving farther out on the ledge. One by one they eased themselves behind him along the rock shelf just as the short man came to the edge of the hole. He reached out his hand and barely missed grabbing Randy's jacket.

"We've got you now," he warned.

The boys had only inched a few steps farther when Jeff slipped on a wet rock. His foot slid off the ledge causing him to completely lose his balance. Without giving it a second thought, Hal grabbed him by one shoulder and Randy clung on to the other.

"Help me get my foot back on the ledge," Jeff whispered in fright.

Hal and Randy held on to him as tightly as they could until Jeff pulled his leg from the side of the drop-off and regained his footing.

"When we catch you, you guys are going to wish you *had* fallen over the side," the thin man announced.

After moving about fifteen or twenty feet more, just like a stubborn mule, Stewart simply stopped.

"I'm so afraid of heights. You guys have no idea."

"I suppose you have claustrophobia too," Jeff taunted.

"What is it?"

"It means you feel like the walls are closing in on you."

"Ohhh, nnno," Stewart moaned.

"We'll add that one to the list," Jeff said. "Now keep moving."

This time he did. Even Stewart was surprised when he made it around to the other side of the hole. Soon the others joined him.

"Shine your lights on the ledge," Randy ordered.

"No way," Stewart objected. "I'm not helping those guys come over here and get me."

It didn't really matter what he said since his helmet lights were lying shattered on the bottom of the endless pit they had just passed. The rest of the boys did as Randy suggested. Stewart reached around in his backpack and pulled out another light which wasn't hard for him to find.

Even Randy was surprised by what happened next.

Chapter 12

First one of the men, then the second, began to move out onto the same ledge the boys had just crossed.

"Keep shining your lights," Randy encouraged.

"That's very kind of you," the thin man said.

"You guys are real gentlemen," the other told them.

After they had gotten half way around the ledge Randy called out, "Off!"

All four lights went out. Randy remembered how he had felt in Sunday school when he opened his eyes in the dark and couldn't see anything. But he had never been anywhere that seemed this black. It was so dark he could almost reach out and feel it.

"Hey! Turn those things back on."

"Yeah, we can't see nothin', and we're stuck out here in the middle of this here ledge."

"That's the way we like it," Jeff said.

"Come on now. If you turn them back on and help us get across, we'll share half the loot with you."

"Right now we have all of it," Stewart reported smugly.

"See, I told you they were the ones that had it," the second man groaned.

Randy told his friends to sit down on the floor. "We need to crawl again so we can get far enough away from those guys that they won't be able to see our lights. Then we can talk."

Once more they began to slowly crawl. Feeling their way they tried hard to rely on their other senses. There was no way to know if other deep holes lay ahead.

"I'm glad I did my report on what lives in a cave or we'd have to be afraid of bears and everything," Stewart remembered. "Now I can see why the things that live back here are blind. I mean what good are your eyes at a time like this?"

The path made a sharp turn to the left, so they knew their lights would no longer be seen by the men on the ledge.

"Let's stop here and take a break," Randy said. "Get out a couple snacks and your water." In silence they sat there resting.

"I'll bet those blind things that live back here are saying, 'Hey, what's the bright idea you guys comin' back here where we live?'" Jeff joked.

"If anything besides the four of us starts talking I'm going to jump up and run for my life," Stewart cried. "It won't matter what else could hurt me then."

"I've been thinking," Randy began. "Maybe we'll have to stay in here till Sunday or Monday. At least my parents know we're in a cave on your uncle's farm, Jeff, but I wish the rest of you had told the truth to your parents. See the kind of problems you can get into when you don't?"

He could sense by their silence that the others knew they hadn't done the right thing.

"Did you guys look at your lesson for Sunday school tomorrow?"

Since Mr. Roberts began teaching their class, they had each wanted to be prepared for the class every Sunday. Even Stewart had read his lesson for this week.

"It's about Joseph's story, remember? At least we didn't fall into a pit like where Joseph was," Randy said.

"It's a good thing too," Stewart added, "or we'd be dead by now."

"Well, the story says that he felt all alone when his brothers put him in that pit. They sold him to be a slave," Randy added.

"Didn't he have to go to prison for almost six years?" Jeff asked.

"Yeah, and then he helped that guy figure out what his dream meant," Hal said.

"God had a plan for Joseph," Randy continued. "He wanted Joseph to know he wasn't all alone. God was with him no matter what."

"I'm glad we're together," Jeff said.

"God knows where we are. Jesus did a lot of miracles, and He can help us get out of this mess too."

"But we're stuck way back here, and those guys are between

us and the only way I know out of here," Stewart complained.

"I know, and all we can do is sit tight and wait. Those guys are going no place any time soon. That's for sure. Our only hope is to wait."

"Then what?" Jeff asked.

"Sooner or later someone has to come looking for us. My dad will probably come out to the farm and ask your uncle where we are."

"But that won't be until tomorrow," Hal noted.

"That's the best we got."

"Wait a minute," Jeff said. "Why didn't I think of it before?"

"What didn't you think of?" Stewart asked.

"There *is* a way out."

"How?"

"That's the secret to this place."

"A secret? What secret?"

"The last time I was out here with my uncle, he was making sure there weren't any hunters on his property."

"So?"

"So we must have walked forever, but we came around this one hill and he pointed to another small opening in the ground."

"You mean there's another way in here?" Hal asked excitedly.

"Yes."

"You mean another way *out* of here, don't you?" Stewart said.

"Right."

"Well, where is it?"

"That's the problem. I only saw it from the outside, and I have no idea where we are right now."

"I remember something from my research," Randy said. "The guy who first found Luray Caverns got up close to the entrance and the wind from the cave blew out his candle."

"Yeah, remember the cold air we felt coming out of *this* place?" Jeff asked.

"That's what I'm talking about. With that much air moving, it has to be coming from someplace. Let's take out our candles."

"Candles? Why candles?" Stewart asked. "I've got a couple hundred pounds of flashlights and batteries and that's all. Hey, Jeff, pass me one of your fruit bars, would ya?"

"If we light the candles, we can see if wind blows on the flame. If it does, then we must be at one end or the other of a tunnel in the ground."

"That's a great idea," Hal said.

They took candles out along with their waterproof matches. Randy gave an extra candle to Stewart. Hal lit his first and the others used it to get theirs going. They held the candles straight up, and it appeared the flames bent slightly in the direction farther around the corner from where they were sitting.

"If we go this way, we might just find another way out of here," Randy pointed. "Then we can get to your uncle's house and call for help."

They must have walked for nearly an hour. Every few minutes they stopped to check which way their flames were pointing.

The farther they went, the more their flames bent over. Then, all at once every candle blew out, and the boys were again plunged into total darkness. As their eyes adjusted from the light their candles had given, Randy noticed that things didn't look as black as before. He looked closer and could make out the faint outline of a wall or rocks just ahead of him. "What's that up ahead?" he asked.

"Don't joke around," Stewart begged.

"No, honest I can see something. Look up there." They looked up, and there was something.

The floor of the cave began to slope upward toward a faint light.

"Turn your lights back on," Jeff said.

With those illuminating the area they were able to move safely up the path.

"Don't forget," Stewart reminded the, "with what you can find around a cave entrance I wouldn't grab on to too many rocks if I were you."

They came to what looked like the end of the path. All that stood in front of them now was a big pile of rocks.

"We need to take our packs off again," Randy told them. "We should be able to crawl over these rocks and see what's on the other side, then pull your pack after you."

Hal went first this time. He crawled up and disappeared over the top. "I think you guys are going to like this. Come on over."

When all four had crawled over, they could see light spilling in from several places.

"There's just a bunch of brush and weeds covering this entrance," Randy said.

The boys cleared a path and safely crawled outside into the sunshine again.

"When we were in Sunday school that light hurt my eyes, but this light feels just fine," Stewart said as he squinted.

Randy thought, *Once I was blind, but now I can see.* "Thank you, Lord," he whispered.

"Let's hurry to my uncle's house," Jeff yelled.

The boys hardly noticed the load they carried on their backs as they ran. Well, Stewart noticed his. Soon they were pounding on the back door of the farmhouse. Jeff's aunt let them in. It wasn't until then that they took a good look at each other. The boys resembled the losing team in the New Market Mud-Wrestling Association. They all started howling and pointing at each other. Randy had never enjoyed laughing so much before in all his life. Somehow they managed to blurt out their story.

Jeff's uncle immediately called the police. Then he went out to the main road to wait for them so he could lead the way to his cave. The boys went back to wait by their campsite until help arrived. It was an amazing sight to see dozens of police cars from the town, county, and state.

"If we had our scanner powered up, it'd be on fire," Jeff said.

"Bet it would've had a meltdown by now," Stewart added. "I wish we could be there to hear it."

"I'd rather be right where we are," Randy said.

Sirens continued to come screaming down the dirt lane in a roaring dust storm right up to the edge of the woods. When the patrol units all stopped, Randy couldn't see a single car until the dust cleared.

An army of police officers gathered together for a short meeting and then stormed off toward the cave with Jeff's uncle leading the charge. About thirty minutes later some of them returned with the two bank robbers in handcuffs, and the police put each in the back seats of different squad cars.

A few minutes later, other officers came out of the woods carrying a big, blue duffel bag and the two shotguns. Those were put into a van marked Crime Investigation Unit.

One of the officers, along with Jeff's uncle, walked over to where the boys sat. "You young men can be very proud of what you did. Without your help we might never have caught up with those guys. You are true heroes."

Heroes. Randy let that word wander around in his thoughts for a minute.

After everything was loaded up, the police drove away.

"Think we'll get a big reward?" Stewart asked.

"We should get at least half the money," Jeff added.

"We're just lucky to get out of that place alive," Randy said. "That's reward enough for me."

"Yeah, but this has to be the biggest thing since the Battle of New Market. They celebrate that every summer, so you can imagine how big *this* is gonna be," Hal suggested.

"Well, if we really are heroes, then how come I don't feel like one?" Randy asked.

Chapter 13

The next week raced by. At church, Mr. Roberts spent the entire hour talking about what had happened. The rest of the kids had a million questions. Then at school all their friends wanted to get close to the town's newest heroes. There was a special assembly held in their honor. It was all just a little too embarrassing.

"We're the same guys you knew last week," Randy pleaded.

The newspaper made special arrangements to take a picture of the boys out in their shed around the scanner. Radio and television stations also sent reporters, and the boys even got a letter signed by the governor.

Back home at the dinner table with his parents, Randy sat playing with the food on his plate.

"What's wrong?" his mother asked. "I made your favorite food and you've hardly touched it."

"Nothing."

"Well, *something* is bothering you," his father said. "What is it?"

"Everybody's trying to tell us what great heroes we are.

The police, the kids at school and church, even the letter from the governor. But it isn't true."

"What do you mean?"

"One of the first things you're supposed to do is tell someone when you go into a cave, and you have to ask permission from the owner."

"We didn't want you to go, but at least you asked us, and we said yes," his mother added.

"I know, but I was the only one who did. It was a scary place, and we're lucky nothing bad happened."

"We don't believe in luck, son," his father said.

"Well, you can't imagine how terrible it was in there. I know God helped us. Only we aren't heroes."

"The newspaper said you might get a reward," his mother informed him.

"We don't deserve it," Randy responded emphatically. He pushed himself away from the table and went to his room.

The next day was Saturday. The mayor arranged a big celebration and the entire town was expected to come out to see them. Randy called the guys and asked them to come over for a special meeting on Friday night. They sat on the back porch to talk about all that had happened.

"Do you guys know they're planning to give us plaques, medals, and a reward?"

"Yeah, I'm so excited I can hardly sleep at night," Stewart said.

Randy just sat there looking down at his feet. "I don't know what to think."

"About what?" Hal asked.

"Everyone is talking about the great heroes we're supposed to be. I don't know. It makes me feel kind of creepy."

"Why?" Jeff asked. "We really *are* heroes. I mean we did help capture the bank robbers, and we helped get the money back for the bank. The president of that place was *real* happy to see us."

"Why don't we put it to a vote?" Hal suggested. "All those who think we're heroes raise your hand."

Three boys voted yes, but Randy didn't put his hand up.

"Randy?"

"I'm just not sure. You guys remember last year when we did our reports for history about the Battle of New Market? A lot of the soldiers from around here were just kids not much older than we are. Those guys were heroes. We just happened to be in the right place at the right time and that's all there is to it."

"Isn't that what a hero is?" Stewart asked. "Aren't they supposed to be people who do the right thing at the right time?"

"Maybe."

"So what's the problem?" Jeff asked.

"The problem is that some of us didn't tell the truth. How can we be heroes if we didn't do that? Plus, we didn't actually catch anybody."

"No?" Stewart countered. "Then who was it that got those

two guys to walk out to the middle of that ledge where they had to wait till help came? Us. That's who."

"All I can tell you is if they plan to go through with giving us a reward, I'm giving mine back," Randy said.

"You can't be serious," Stewart scoffed.

"I *am* serious. You can do what you want with yours, but I'm not keeping mine."

There wasn't any reason to take a vote this time. The choice was up to each one of them individually. It was the kind of decision no one can make for another person because it had to come from the inside.

The town made elaborate plans for a celebration. Early the next morning, media people came from all over the region. There was a rumor that even the governor might be coming to hand out the medals and citations in person. Randy hadn't been this nervous since the incident back in the cave.

The schedule set the ceremony for eleven-thirty at the gazebo outside City Hall. Randy's father decided they would drive over, but this proved to be a mistake. As he tried to back out of the driveway, cars were already parking along both sides of their street.

"I think we'd better walk," he suggested. "With our car in the garage, we're already closer than most people are going to be able to park."

Randy wondered if anyone would recognize him on the street now that he had to walk out there in plain sight. His picture was already plastered all over the paper, and his interview had run on television.

He wasn't sure, but Randy thought someone just snapped another picture of him. "Can we walk faster?" he begged.

The family came to the end of the block and turned toward City Hall. Randy couldn't believe the spectacle. There were cars, trucks, and people everywhere. He still didn't know how much money had been in that bag, but now he was beginning to think it must have been a lot.

Randy had never seen so many people in his town. Every year the Civil War reenactment of the battle drew thousands of visitors, but that was nothing like the number of people who had come today.

When the family reached City Hall, they saw an area was roped off so that most people had to stay back. A policeman saw Randy's family coming and escorted them to some special seats right in front. The other guys had already arrived with their families.

For nearly twenty minutes several people came up to a microphone and made speeches. After each one, the crowd clapped and cheered. Then it came time for the governor to make his speech. As he went to the podium, two assistants carried boxes and placed them on a table.

"Think the reward money is in those?" Stewart whispered.

"Shhhh," his mother reprimanded.

Then, one at a time, the governor called each boy up to the platform. As they shook hands, one assistant placed a medal around the boy's neck while another official handed him a plaque. The bank president was last in line, and he gave them each an envelope. Then each boy returned to his parents who sat proudly in front of the whole town.

Randy was the last to be called up.

"I understand," announced the governor, "that Randy, here, is president of a detective club. From what I've been told, he's the one who came up with the plan to capture the thieves. I wonder if you'd like to say a few words, son."

Now, Randy really became nervous. His heart started pounding, he felt light-headed, and it was difficult to catch his breath. He wasn't sure if he was about to pass out or what, but he made it up to the microphone somehow. Even as he stood there, his legs buckled beneath him, threatening to give out at any second. A man came over and lowered the stand so the crowd could hear Randy. Everyone appeared very interested in what he had to say. Right then, Randy was too.

"I want to thank all of you for coming today."

He looked down at his parents. Their faces beamed with pride.

"I want to thank you for these things you've given us today."

The crowd cheered and clapped.

When the sound subsided, Randy spoke again, "But I have to say something."

"Here it comes," Stewart sighed.

"There have been a lot of people who want to call us heroes."

That drew the wildest, longest, loudest cheer of the morning.

The crowd began to chant, "He-roes! He-roes! He-roes!"

Randy held his hands up to ask for quiet.

"It wasn't all that long ago when some terrible things happened to our country. With Washington D.C so close to where we live, it affected people in our town more than in some others. I know it bothered me a lot. Sometimes when my parents saw certain things on TV, they'd start to cry."

Randy looked down to see tears streaming down his mother's cheeks. His father tried hard, but he had to wipe his eyes too. Randy looked around and people he didn't even know were also crying. That choked him up a little. He cleared his throat a couple times and continued.

"I think we get things all twisted up sometimes about what's important and what isn't. I don't feel like a hero no matter what anyone else says. I just don't. To me, the real heroes were the men who drove their police cars out into the middle of nowhere, went into a dark, dangerous cave, and brought those two men out. Police officers, firemen, ambulance drivers . . . they do things like that all the time. We hardly give it any thought. That's why we formed our club so we could learn more about them. I think I might want to do something like they do when I grow up."

The crowd stood silent. The only sound came from an American and a Virginian flag flapping together in the wind at the top of tall flagpoles right next to where Randy was standing.

"So, anyway, I've decided to donate my reward money to the real heroes, the people who look out for us every day. I'm going to ask my dad to help me figure out how to do it."

He took the envelope he had been handed by the bank president and placed it on the podium in front of him.

"I don't want you to think I'm not thankful, but I'd like to give the money back."

"That's a five thousand dollar check," the mayor whispered.

Randy looked out and saw his three friends get up out of their seats. They walked to the front of the crowd and placed their envelopes on the podium . . . except for Stewart. He stood up there for the longest time just looking down at his. Then, reluctantly, he added it to the pile. Again the crowd cheered, even louder and longer than before.

Later that afternoon the guys met for their regular weekly meeting back at the shed. Jeff stood up and announced,

"As a member of the Hilton Park Road Detective Club I hereby declare the meeting open. First order of business will be to vote on the question, "Is Randy Wilcox totally out of his mind?" Everyone laughed.

"I can't believe we gave it back," Hal groaned.

"Me neither," Stewart added. "My Mom still can't figure it out."

"I'm not sure I can either," Randy sighed. Before anyone could say another word their scanner picked up a radio transmission about an accident right in the center of town. It wasn't serious, but the dispatcher alerted an ambulance just to be safe.

Randy looked at the scanner then turned back to the guys. "I'm sure glad those people are out there."

"Me too," Jeff added.

Hal stood to his feet, "All those who agree, raise your hand."

Everyone did.

The End

Hampton, Virginia 10-Codes and Fire Signals

10-1   Call Headquarters

10-2   Location

10-3   Report To Headquarters

10-4   Message Received

10-5   Coffee Break

10-6   Lunch Break

10-7   Off Duty

10-8   On Duty

10-9   Investigating Vehicle/Occupant

10-10 Drunk Driver

10-11 Out Of Service-HQS

10-12 Out Of Service-Court

10-14 Suspicious Person/Vehicle

10-15 Person Armed

10-16 Vehicle License Info

10-17 Auto Accident-Property Damage

10-18 Auto Accident-Injury

10-19 Auto Accident-Fatal

10-20 Ambulance

10-21 Wrecker

10-22 Out Of Service (Location)

10-23 Hit & Run—Property Damage

10-24 Hit & Run—Injury

10-25 Hit & Run—Fatal

10-26 Jail Break—All Cars

10-27 Officer Needs Help

10-28 Fight/Disturbance

10-29 Illegally Parked Vehicle

10-30 Prowler

10-31 Racing/Speeding (location)

10-32 Disorderly Person (s)

10-33 Vandalism

10-34 At Headquarters W/Prisoner

10-35 Arrived At Scene

10-36 Warrant

10-37 See Complainant

10-38 Fire

10-39 Meet Officer

10-40 Traffic Stop

10-41 Repeat

10-42 Time

10-43 Finished Assignment

10-44 Remain In Service

10-45 Loud Party

10-46 Computer Terminal Down

10-47 Prisoner

10-48 Radar

10-49 Escort (location)

10-50 Stand-By

10-51 Not On File

10-52 Time Call-All Cars

10-53 Confidential Assignment

10-54 Blood Relay

10-55 Emergency Message

10-56 Cancellation

10-57 Abandoned Vehicle

10-58 Contact By Phone

10-59 Larceny

10-60 Breaking & Entering

10-61 Stolen Vehicle

10-62 Narcotics Violation

10-63 Overdose

10-65 Unwanted Guest

10-66 Bomb Threat

10-67 Deceased Person

10-68 Suicide

10-69 Homicide

10-70 Juvenile

10-71 Open Door (location)

10-72 Open Window (location)

10-73 Drowning

10-74 Runaway

10-75 Out Of Service-Jail

10-76 Out Of Service-Garage

10-77 Out Of Service-Gas Pump

10-78 Flat Tire

10-79 Police Car Accident

10-80 Dead Animal (location)

10-81 Barking Dog

10-82 Street Sign Down (location)

10-83 Disabled Vehicle (location)

10-84 Traffic Light Malfunction

10-85 Lost Child

10-86 Escaped Prisoner

10-87 Kidnapping

10-88 Contact Chief's Office

10-89 Confidential Information

10-90 Personal Relief

10-91 Breathalyzer Needed

10-92 Burgular Alarm

10-93 Armed Robbery (location)

10-94 Mentally Disturbed Person

10-95 Arson (location)

10-96 Tower Light Check (car no.)

10-97 Contact Coroner

10-98 ID Officer Requested

10-99 Taxi Requested (location)

FIRE SIGNALS:

0 Minor Nature

1 Additional Manpower Needed

2 Second Alarm

3 Third Alarm

4 Need Utility Truck

5 Need Ladder Truck

6 Need Water Truck

7 Need Pumper

8 Need Ambulance

9 Need Foam Truck

10 Need Civil Defense Truck

11 Notify Chief/Marshall

12 Notify City Manager

13 Request Police Works

14 Request Coroner

15 Request Virgina Power (elect.)

16 Request Virgina Natural Gas

17 Police Needed

FIRE CODES:

RED——Flames Showing

BLACK—Smoke Showing

WHITE—Nothing Showing